"Everybody needs reminding sometimes that time can be short," Hanna said. "And that it's important to make the most of it. Especially when you're only going to be somewhere for a day or two."

Oh…man… He'd always been quite sure he was immune to being seduced. That he could stay completely in control at all times. It seemed that that assumption might be incorrect.

And in this moment, Mac couldn't have cared less.

But he could see a flash of what looked like vulnerability in those amazing eyes. Because Hanna was offering an invitation that might be rejected?

As if…

He could take at least an element of control back, couldn't he? And let her rest assured that her invitation was more than welcome. In his mind, it didn't really matter who initiated that kiss because it seemed they both wanted it just as much as each other. As Hanna's lips parted beneath his and he felt the exquisite touch of her tongue against his, Mac gave up overthinking any of this.

There were no rules.

Time was indeed short and they should both absolutely make the most of it.

Dear Reader,

I suspect every one of us has been affected in many ways by the global pandemic. I really miss the freedom to travel, but I'm also aware of how lucky I've already been to visit some of Europe's most beautiful cities.

One of my all-time favorites has to be Prague, and I realized I could go there again by writing a story that included not only the unique features of an astonishing city but its inherent romance as well. So that's where Hanna and Mac meet—in front of the famous astronomical clock in the Old Town Square. They have their weekend in Prague. They also have a few days in Barcelona, which is another favorite for me, and then I swap Europe for New Zealand because the growing love between them is irresistible enough to cross the world for.

Come traveling with Hanna and Mac. The journey, both actual and emotional, was such a pleasure for me to write and I really hope it will be just as much of a pleasure for you to read.

With love,

Alison xx

ONE WEEKEND
IN PRAGUE

ALISON ROBERTS

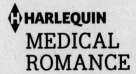

HARLEQUIN
MEDICAL
ROMANCE

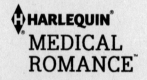

HARLEQUIN®
MEDICAL
ROMANCE™

Recycling programs
for this product may
not exist in your area.

ISBN-13: 978-1-335-73733-5

One Weekend in Prague

Copyright © 2022 by Alison Roberts

For questions and comments about the quality of this book,
please contact us at CustomerService@Harlequin.com.

Harlequin Enterprises ULC
22 Adelaide St. West, 41st Floor
Toronto, Ontario M5H 4E3, Canada
www.Harlequin.com

Printed in U.S.A.

Alison Roberts has been lucky enough to live in the South of France for several years recently but is now back in her home country of New Zealand. She is also lucky enough to write for the Harlequin Medical Romance line. A primary school teacher in a former life, she later became a qualified paramedic. She loves to travel and dance, drink champagne, and spend time with her daughter and her friends. Alison Roberts is the author of over one hundred books!

Books by Alison Roberts

Harlequin Medical Romance

Two Tails Animal Refuge
The Vet's Unexpected Family

Royal Christmas at Seattle General
Falling for the Secret Prince

A Surgeon with a Secret
Unlocking the Rebel's Heart
Stolen Nights with the Single Dad
Christmas Miracle at the Castle
Miracle Baby, Miracle Family
A Paramedic to Change Her Life

Visit the Author Profile page
at Harlequin.com for more titles.

Praise for
Alison Roberts

"Ms. Roberts has delivered a delightful read in this book where the chemistry between this couple was strong from the moment they meet...[and] the romance was heart-warming."

CHAPTER ONE

OH... HOW AMAZING WAS this?

It was late enough to be dark on a summer's night and Hanna Peterson was somewhere she'd never been before in her life. Somewhere so magical, the views from the taxi windows seemed like glimpses of a fantasy city as the driver negotiated busy roads and narrow streets to take them into the ancient centre of Prague.

'I can't believe this,' she said, turning her head to where her best friend, Jo, was sitting in the back seat of the taxi. 'I feel like I've stepped into a fairy tale.'

Everywhere Hanna looked, there was something astonishing. Lights gilded the spires of Prague's famous castle on the hill and all the statues that guarded the length of the bridge leading over to that side of the river. There were cobbled streets and squares and every building looked unique. Dramatic in their extravagant architecture, mysterious in their antiquity and, oh, so romantic with their myriad rooflines of steep slopes and domes and spires stretching into the night sky.

'Mmm…' But Jo wasn't looking out of the windows right now. She was resting her head on the shoulder of the man sitting beside her, gazing up adoringly at her new husband, Cade. 'Me, too…'

Hanna shook her head. 'I also can't believe I've crashed your honeymoon. I feel like the biggest gooseberry ever.'

Jo sat up. Slowly. In the last trimester of her pregnancy, the long international flight had been more uncomfortable than usual. 'Don't be silly,' she said. 'You're not on our *whole* honeymoon. We just happen to be all going to the same conference for the weekend. Then Cade and I will go to the nearest beach where I'll lie there like the beached whale I am for another day or two and you'll go off on one of your adventures.' She put her head back on Cade's shoulder. 'Anyway, this could be seen as a babymoon instead of a honeymoon.'

Cade laughed. 'Wouldn't you have a babymoon *after* the baby arrives, like a honey-moon is after the wedding?'

'Are you kidding?' Hanna grinned. 'Nobody gets a holiday after a baby arrives. You'll be dreaming of having one. For years and years and years…'

It was easy to tap into the jokes. The ones that emphasised that Hanna had never wanted kids. Or a husband, for that matter, because they tended to want the ankle-biters that stopped you going on holidays.

Mind you, she'd never seen Jo look this happy. She'd been the bridesmaid and witness at the private wedding ceremony, just a few days ago, on a beach near Dunedin in the South Island of New Zealand and, despite the incredibly long journey to get to this part of Europe and how tired Jo had to be, she was still glowing with the joy of it all.

Hanna turned back to stare out of the window again, partly because she didn't want to miss anything but it was also to distract herself from that twinge of something she didn't like.

Envy? Surely not. But there was something niggling deep down that was disturbing and it had started when she'd been standing on that beach, watching Jo and Cade exchange vows. It seemed to get slightly sharper edges every time she caught the way they looked at each other, too, so maybe it was best to keep looking at the enticing view outside. She'd be able to appreciate it even more tomorrow when she went on that walking tour she'd booked online as soon as she'd known she was coming here.

The tour was the only thing Hanna had booked for the next three weeks, apart from her flights. She'd always loved to follow her nose and make impetuous decisions when it came to travel because the very best discoveries and adventures could be found that way. And, if they turned out to be disappointing, she could just change her plans instantly and try something else. She hadn't been on an overseas trip for more than a year and Hanna could feel the tendrils of a familiar and very welcome excitement flickering with enough strength to make that niggle disappear.

Maybe this trip to Prague and whatever awaited her after the intensive two days at the conference was a timely reminder that being single and childfree was the ticket to the most amazing, memorable adventures. It always had been, after all.

* * *

Hamish MacMillan had unpacked his toilet bag but he took a moment to make sure he hadn't forgotten anything.

His toothbrush was in the glass the hotel had provided on the shelf above the basin, wearing its plastic cap to keep clean, accompanied by toothpaste and floss. His hairbrush and comb were beside the glass. With a satisfied nod, Mac noted that his shaving kit was ready for use first thing tomorrow morning and walked back into the lavish bedroom in a rather wonderful hotel in the Old Town Square in Prague.

His shirts hung neatly in the wardrobe already, along with a smart, pinstriped suit and a small selection of ties. The more casual clothing, which he could wear when he wasn't being a keynote speaker at a prestigious international medical conference, could stay in his suitcase for now. Mac had a laptop bag with other things he needed to check before he could finally get to bed.

Important things, like the USB stick that had the transcript and images that went with the presentation he would be giving to open this two-day conference on Emergency Medicine. It also had a folder containing all his arrangements for the holiday he had planned to fill in the week between this speaking engagement and the next one, which was in Paris. The prospect of a few days of some early summer warmth in Europe had been so much more appealing than flying back to his home in Scotland that had been closed up for over a year and would, no doubt, be about as inviting as walking into an over-sized refrigerator.

It had been a pleasure to find a luxury bus tour where every detail of accommodation, transport and meals was prearranged. Mac would be able not only to enjoy exploring places he either loved or had never visited but also genuinely relax knowing that he could rely on the organisation skills of others to make sure everything would run smoothly.

Registration instructions for the conference were also in the folder but the main desk wouldn't open until tomorrow afternoon. That left an entire morning and Mac intended to make the most of it. He was on his first visit to a city with a fascinating history and he wanted to learn as much as possible but where would be the best place to start?

Probably right here in front of his hotel, he decided, and the thought prompted him to abandon the plan to fire up his laptop and scroll through the conference programme to see what he might like to listen to. Instead, he went to the doors set inside the arched window of his room and stepped out onto the balcony. It was completely dark now but the square was humming with life. There were people walking, sitting on the steps of a huge, central monument and crowding outdoor restaurants and bars. The spires of ornate churches and facades of other buildings were bathed in spotlights and there were vehicles pulling up to hotel entrances.

A taxi had just stopped in front of this hotel and Mac's gaze caught briefly as he watched a man holding out his hand to help a woman from the back seat of the car. A rather heavily pregnant woman. A third passenger was already out of the car. Another woman, but this one was tall and slim and had a long braid of hair hanging down the line of her spine. There was something about her that caught his attention. Perhaps it was the way she seemed oblivious to her companions or the luggage the taxi driver was hauling from the boot. She was staring at

something, utterly entranced. The churches?
No…maybe it was that building almost directly opposite the hotel. The one with the
chunky tower that had a crowd of people
gathered in front of it.

Mac didn't need to hear the chiming of
a clock to know what was happening. And
a glance at his watch told him why people
had gathered. He'd learned about the famous
astronomical clock when he was no more
than ten years old and he'd fallen totally in
love with it. That clock had probably been
the main incentive to accept the invitation
to speak at this particular conference but it
had been pushed firmly to the back of his
mind as he'd dealt with the logistics of finding his hotel and unpacking.

A curious sensation was growing in Mac's
gut as he took in the chimes fading and heard
the faint sound of clapping and cheers from
across the large square, but it took a moment
to recognise that it might be excitement. A
kind of excitement that made him a little
nervous, to be honest, because memories of
feeling like this told him that this feeling
could morph into fear in a heartbeat. That
the feeling that something amazing might be
about to happen wasn't to be trusted.

The woman with the braid turned away from the view and looked up at the hotel. Mac knew she couldn't see him but he could see her quite clearly. Clearly enough to see the expression on her face that told him she totally trusted that feeling. That she had absolute confidence that something amazing was already happening and that she was going to enjoy every moment of it.

Mac found himself smiling as he went back into his room. He opened up his laptop but, instead of finding the conference programme to study, or the contact details of people he needed to liaise with for his own commitments to that programme, he typed a query into the subject line of the search bar.

Tours that include the astronomical clock in Prague

He clicked on one that promised to cover the main attractions of Prague in a two-hour period and chose the earliest time for tomorrow morning. It was a walking tour that started right in front of the clock, which sounded like a perfect way to start his day. Eight-forty a.m. seemed an unusually precise time to start a tour but that only made it more attractive and, with a satisfied nod, Mac booked himself in.

Hanna had to run across the square to make it in time because the lace on her most comfortable sneakers had broken. Fortunately, Jo was going to rest this morning, so she'd pulled a lace from one of her trainers and lent it to Hanna. Also fortunately, it was obvious who the guide was, because he was holding up a red flag with a white 'W' on it. Hanna arrived just in time to hear the middle-aged man explaining that the letter was not only because this was a walking tour but that his name was William.

'Welcome to Prague, ladies and gentlemen. It will be my pleasure to introduce you all to the beautiful capital of the Czech Republic, also known as the City of a Hundred Spires. Prague is my home and my native language is Czech and, while this tour is in English, I'm also fluent in French and German. How many of you have English as your first language?'

Hanna cast a quick glance around the group of about a dozen people, noting that only half of them were raising their hands along with her. A man at the front, who was very tall and had a commendably good posture, turned as if he was wondering the same thing and, weirdly, when he saw Hanna his eyes widened as if he recognised her.

He must be mistaking her for someone else, she thought, because if she'd met *him* before she'd certainly remember it. It wasn't simply his height or posture that would make him stand out in a crowd, he was immaculately dressed in a short-sleeved, open-necked white shirt and well-fitting khaki chinos and his face was…distinctive. A bit craggy, with deep lines from his nose to the corners of his mouth and eyes that—even at this distance and for only the space of a heartbeat—gave her the impression that he was examining whatever he could see with great care.

Hurriedly, Hanna tuned back into what William was saying. 'We are standing in the Old Town Square and, as I'm sure you're all aware, we're standing in front of one of the most popular tourist attractions in Prague—our medieval astronomical clock or the Prague Orloj.' He checked his watch. 'In fifteen minutes it will provide its animated hourly show of the apostles' march and that gives me just enough time to tell you a few things about it. Let's get a little closer so that we'll have the best view.'

William smiled at Hanna and she got the impression he'd seen her running across the cobbled square to get here in time. She smiled back as she moved with the group to stand as close as possible to both the clock and their guide. Hanna ended up at the front of the group on the opposite side to the tall man in chinos and she found her gaze drifting sideways shortly after William started talking again.

'The clock was installed early in the fifteenth century,' he told them. 'Legend has it that, when it was completed, the clock maker was blinded by the city councillors to prevent him making a better clock for any other city. In return, it is said that he ended his life by throwing himself into the workings of the clock to damage it and he put a curse on anyone who tried to repair it. They say it didn't work for a hundred years after that.'

The grim story had certainly caught everyone's attention but Hanna was still watching the man as he gave a slow nod, as if he thought that was fair enough, and Hanna found herself suppressing a smile. He was staring up at the large, ornate dials on the tower wall, clearly fascinated by what was obviously a mechanical and mathematical triumph, but Hanna wasn't concentrating on what William was telling them about how the positions of the sun and moon were shown or which medallions represented months of the year. She was simply taking in the moment and letting that bubble of excitement in her belly grow, knowing that this was the first step of her new adventure.

Which was probably why it took a moment longer than it might have to realise that something wasn't quite right.

'The four figures you can see at each side of the clock are representations of things that were the most despised.' William was rubbing his forehead, his expression suggesting he was in pain. 'The man on the left is…is admiring himself in a mirror. This is…' William paused as if he'd forgotten what he was about to say and, when he did say something, it made no sense whatsoever.

The prickle of awareness Hanna could feel was something that could only be developed from years of experience in dealing with medical emergencies. Something physical was interfering with William's ability to think. It could be something like a

very low blood sugar in a person with dia-
betes but the worst-case scenario would be
that he was having a stroke where a blocked
or burst blood vessel could be starting to
cause catastrophic damage. That would explain him looking as if he'd had a sudden
onset headache.

Poised to move to his side, for some reason, Hanna took a heartbeat to look across
at the tall man and his head turned at exactly the same moment. There was recog-
nition there. They were both on high alert.
They both knew that something was about
to happen.

And happen it did. Even as they both
moved forward in the same instant, their
guide crumpled, his head striking the cobbled ground with a sickening crunch. A few
seconds later and his body began convuls-
ing in a full tonic-clonic seizure.

Hanna's first action was to scan the immediate surroundings for any object that needed
to be moved. William had already injured his
head—she could see it was bleeding—and
they needed to prevent any further injuries.
She picked up the metal pole with the red
flag on the top and handed it to someone
behind her.

'Please move back,' she requested. 'We need some space.'

A glance sideways showed her that the tall man had his phone out but he wasn't speaking to call an ambulance and Hanna knew that he was most likely activating the stopwatch function to record both the time of onset of the seizure and how long it lasted.

It was certainly not showing any signs of stopping yet. Above them, the clock was now in motion with a tinny, repetitive chiming sound that had the effect of ramping up the tension of this situation. So did the press of people around them, staring in horror at the sight of William's head still bumping against the ground. Hanna looked around. She needed to put something between William's skull and the unforgiving cobbles. Preferably an article of clothing that was thicker than the soft, peasant-style blouse she was wearing over a camisole, although she was starting to pull it off already.

'Here, use this.' The man had a pullover draped over his shoulders. 'It should provide enough protection.'

He had a Scottish accent but Hanna was more impressed with his manner of speaking and the effortless way he was taking charge of this situation. He folded the soft woollen garment and eased it under William's head. There was nothing more they could do now, other than to protect the man from any further injuries as they waited for the seizure to finish. That wasn't the opinion of others in the small crowd around them, however, which was understandable because it was distressing to hear the sound of abnormal breathing from their tour guide and see skin colour changes from the lack of circulating oxygen.

'We need something to put in his mouth.' The man shouting loudly had an American accent. 'Someone got a spoon? Or a pen? A toothbrush, even? He's going to swallow his tongue and die if we don't do something.'

Hanna's companion raised his voice to be heard above the chiming of more church bells in the square but his tone was perfectly calm. 'It's not possible for someone to swallow their tongue,' he said. 'And we know what we're doing. I'm a doctor.' He glanced at Hanna.

'ED nurse,' she told him.

He gave a single, approving nod, his glance shifting to his phone. 'We need to call an ambulance,' he said. 'He's injured himself and I can't see any medic alert bracelet, can you?'

'No.' William's wrists were bare but Hanna checked inside the top of his shirt for a necklace. 'A lot of people who have epilepsy choose not to wear one, though.'

'It could also be a first seizure.'

It was Hanna's turn to nod. If it was a first seizure, it could be a symptom of something seriously wrong in William's brain, like a tumour.

'Could someone call an ambulance, please?' he called. 'And move back a little more, please. Let's give this man a bit of privacy.'

Nobody had taken any notice of Hanna asking them to move back but this man's calm request had everybody shifting and she got the distinct impression that he could probably take command of any situation without being ignored or challenged. Some people on the edge of the group even turned to walk away and she could hear the call going out for an ambulance.

'How do you say "ambulance" in…?' The man who'd asked for a spoon was still louder than anyone else. 'What is it they speak here?'

'Czech,' someone else said.

'*Záchranka,*' someone else called. 'I've got a translation app.'

'It's on the way, already.' A local policeman was pushing through the onlookers. 'Can I be of assistance?'

The jerking of William's limbs had stopped. He was breathing normally again but was still unconscious. Hanna helped the doctor to put him into a recovery position, crossing one arm over his body and using his shoulder and hip to turn him. She automatically bent his leg to provide more stability, shifted the arm trapped underneath his body and then tilted his head back to ensure his airway was open.

The sound of a siren was already close and an airhorn was being used to clear pedestrians as the vehicle approached. The policemen helped translate information about the event and the length of time the seizure had lasted. The paramedic team were efficient, and William was conscious but confused, with his head bandaged, as they made him comfortable on a stretcher and then loaded him into the ambulance. Spectators dispersed quickly after that with the loud tourist expressing his disappointment.

'Well, so much for that walking tour,' he said. 'I wonder if we can get a refund?'

Others shook their heads and the group rapidly dispersed, leaving Hanna and the doctor alone. He was stooping to pick up his jumper from the cobbles.

'Don't do that,' she said.

'Sorry?' His eyebrows rose sharply at her command.

'It's got blood on it.'

'Yes, I know. But I can hardly leave it here, can I?'

'I've got a bag.' Hanna fished in her shoulder bag to take out a small ball. Releasing the string, she unfolded the reusable shopping bag made of parachute fabric. 'It'll keep you safer.'

'Thanks. I can get it back to you later.' He folded the jumper inwards so that he didn't touch any bloodstains. 'We're staying in the same hotel.'

Hanna blinked. How on earth did he know that?

Her astonishment was clearly visible. 'I saw you arrive last night,' he added. 'Given that you're an ED nurse, I'm guessing you're attending the conference?'

'Yes.' Hanna couldn't hide her smile. 'I'm really looking forward to it.'

Maybe, a small part of that pleasure was

due to the thought that not only had this man taken notice of her arrival last night but he'd remembered her today. That explained why he'd given the impression that he knew who she was when she'd arrived at the tour group's meeting spot.

Her smile faded. 'This morning was my best chance to learn something about Prague, though. I was looking forward to this tour, as well.'

'Me, too.' He was giving her that look again, his eyes very slightly narrowed as if to focus on something important. 'Perhaps we could complete it ourselves? I printed out the itinerary and a map. I'm sure the news-agent stall over there would be able to provide a guidebook that would give us some information about each of the destinations.'

'That's a great idea.' Hanna was smiling again. 'So much better than trying to do it by yourself. My name's Hanna, by the way. Hanna Peterson.'

'I'm Hamish MacMillan,' he told her. 'But I've been called Mac all my adult life.'

The nickname suited him. It was unmis-takeably Scottish as a name but it also suited how tidy this man looked. Buttoned up?

'You're not related to the raincoat people, are you?'

It was his turn to blink as he processed what she meant but then he smiled. 'It's a Mackintosh raincoat, not a MacMillan,' he said. 'There are many names in Scotland that start with a Mc or a Mac.'

It was the first time Hanna had seen this man smile and, for just a heartbeat, she forgot about everything else. It wasn't just that she could *see* his smile. She could *feel* it— filling her head and then sneaking down to curl itself around her heart. And it didn't stop there. It kept going down, to pool somewhere deep in her abdomen where, by some mysterious alchemy, it started to generate heat. She had to drag her gaze away from his smile but she only managed to lift it to where she found a pair of very dark eyes locked onto hers.

Oh, *my*...

Hanna might have to tap into her experience of dealing with potential emergencies again if she was going to be able to speak without revealing any effects of feeling completely blindsided by an attraction that was far more than anything she'd ever experienced in her life.

Oddly, it felt like Mac knew what was going on. Perhaps, by some miracle, this feeling was mutual but, if it was, he was an expert in hiding how he felt.

'Destination One,' he said, waving his hand at the clock above them. 'Prague's famous astronomical clock. Something I've always wanted to see but, somehow—' his tone was deadpan '—I could never find the time…'

Hanna gave a huff of laughter. 'I see what you did there.'

So he had a sense of humour on top of being the most gorgeous man she'd ever seen? Her level of anticipation for what this latest adventure in her life could possibly deliver had just gone through the roof.

'We've got time now,' she said. 'Let's not waste a minute of it.'

CHAPTER TWO

WALKING BACK FROM the newsagent's kiosk, a guidebook in his hand, Mac came to the conclusion that whatever it had been that had captured his attention about this woman last night was even more intense at close range.

He couldn't quite put his finger on what it was, but he suspected it had something to do with her sheer vitality. The energy that she was radiating. She was a hundred per cent involved in what she was experiencing, and he got the impression that Hanna Peterson wanted total immersion in whatever was going on around her. To combine using all her senses but also to learn whatever she could. The curious mind of an intelligent person could be more attractive than a physical feature. Not that Hanna was lacking in physical attractiveness, mind you. Quite the opposite.

Her curious mind had had enough of the

clock, however. When he'd stopped in front of it again, opening his guidebook to find any information other than what William had been able to tell them, she had given him a look that made him laugh out loud.

'You remind me of a dog I saw in Central Park recently,' he told her.

'Well, thanks very much.' Hanna was doing her best to look, and sound, highly offended.

'Not in a bad way,' Mac assured her. 'The dog was trying so hard to sit still but he was desperate to be let off his lead to run.'

Her lips twitched. She wanted to laugh. She was trying hard not to.

'It was a beautiful dog,' Mac added. 'It had a lovely, shiny coat.'

That did it. Her mouth curved into the most delightful grin and there was a sparkle in her eyes that made that hazel green colour come alive within a very distinctive dark rim. With the sun reaching past the spires of the Old Town now, the light made her skin look as delicate as porcelain and the smattering of freckles across her nose and cheekbones was as captivating as the fiery tones of her hair.

Yes, she was undoubtedly physically beautiful. And very smart. But Mac knew there was something else about her that was pulling him in like some kind of magnetic force.

Something irresistible.

'Woof,' Hanna said. 'And you're right. Can you throw the ball, please and take me to destination number two?'

Mac consulted the map and then nodded. 'Follow me.'

It was only a few minutes' walk from the Old Town Square to the Charles Bridge, which had been the next destination on the walking tour. He could understand that Hanna had already ticked the astronomical clock off the list of city highlights. He knew that very few people would have the same fascination for it that he had. He couldn't help throwing a last glance over his shoulder as they headed out of the square.

'You really do have a thing for that clock,' Hanna observed.

'I do,' Mac confessed. 'I blame it on the documentary I saw on telly when I was about nine years old. I was absolutely riveted.'

Hanna's glance was curious. Impressed, even. 'I'm pretty sure I was still watching cartoons when I was that age,' she told him. 'Were you a child genius?'

'Hardly. I just got mesmerised by its complexity, I guess.'

He could remember how enthralled he'd been at the precision of so many working parts, never missing a beat, as they did exactly what they were supposed to do. They were so controlled. Predictable. Dependable. It had been a glimpse into a concept that was alien in an unpredictable life that had the potential to veer across a spectrum with utter neglect at one end and terrifying violence at the other.

Not that he was about to tell a stranger anything about that. It was so far in his past that he didn't need to think about it himself but that wouldn't stop him coming back to have a private moment with that clock before he left this city. A quiet celebration of having achieved some of that predictability and control in his own life?

He was channelling some of that control now, as he cleared his throat and put on his best 'tour guide' voice.

'So, here we have one of Prague's most loved attractions, the Charles Bridge. Completed in 1402, it links the Old Town with the Lesser Town across the Vltava River.

You can see the fortifications of the towers at each end.'

'I can…' Hanna was gazing up at the tall, intricately decorated stone construction with its impossibly steep roof and small spires that was the entrance to the bridge at this end.

'The book says it's one of the most beautiful gothic gateways in the world.'

'I love it.'

Mac could see that she loved it. Her face was glowing with the kind of wonder you might see when a small child was almost overwhelmed with something that amazed them. The way he'd felt when he'd seen that documentary about the clock. When was the last time Mac had felt like that? Too many years to count, that was how many. Because, when you felt like that, you could get pulled in an unexpected direction and well…he wasn't even going to think about what had happened the last time he'd allowed that to happen.

'Would you like to climb the one hundred and thirty-eight steps to the viewing platform?'

'I'd love to.' But the way Hanna then screwed up her nose contradicted her enthusiasm. It also made Mac think of a rabbit sniffing the air to identify an unseen threat and it was…seriously cute. 'But we haven't got that much time and it looks like there's already quite a queue.'

Mac nodded his approval. They had a plan and they needed to stick to a timetable. 'Let's walk across the bridge. I can see the castle already and that's destination number three.'

Hanna's smile had all the anticipation of that small child again, this time waiting to open a Christmas gift, perhaps. It was impossible not to take pleasure in seeing the joy this exploration was giving her. Like the parent of that child, he was able to see something with a perspective that was both poignant and refreshing.

'There are thirty statues of saints,' he told her, scanning the text in the book as they walked. 'And the most famous of all is the first one that was installed. St John of Nepomuk. Apparently, if you touch the statue, it will bring you good luck.'

'Cool.' Hanna tossed him another one of those smiles that lit up her face. 'We should all collect as much good luck as possible. You never know what's just around the next corner, do you?'

'No…that's very true.' Mac was smiling back at her. This time yesterday, he certainly hadn't known that he was going to meet one of the most intriguing women ever. Definitely one of the most attractive. How inappropriate was it, having only met Hanna a matter of minutes ago, that part of his brain was wondering whether kissing her might also be a one-of-a-kind experience?

'I mean, poor William.' Hanna paused for a moment, between the statues and the trestle tables of vendors selling all sorts of tourist friendly items. 'I do hope he's not about to find out something nasty, like that seizure is the first sign of a brain tumour.'

Mac had to wonder if Hanna had any idea how much of what she was feeling was showing on her face and in the tone of her voice. He'd worked with enough people in situations that were sometimes devastating and his instincts were telling him that Hanna was a very genuine person. Compassionate to the point where she possibly became too involved with the patients she treated? Oddly, he felt a note of concern for her—as if her mental wellbeing was important to him.

He shook off the strange sensation by

changing the subject after no more than a murmur of agreement.

'I'm still trying to place your accent,' he said. 'You're not Canadian, are you?'

'Nope.' Hanna was looking down at the river below them.

'Australian?'

'Getting warmer. Hot, even…' The glance he caught was teasing. 'You must have heard of my hometown. It's supposed to be the most Scottish city outside of Scotland.'

'You're from New Zealand,' Mac said, his steps slowing. 'I don't believe it…'

Hanna's eyebrows rose. 'Why is that so surprising? We're known as a nation of travellers. I suspect you'd be able to find a Kiwi in almost any corner of the globe.'

'I know. It's just…a coincidence, I guess.'

'Why?'

'My sister grew up there.' The words were out of Mac's mouth before he remembered that he never told anybody such personal information. 'My twin…'

It was Hanna's turn to look astonished. And Mac could see something else in her gaze, as she processed what hadn't been said, that looked like…what, concern? He got the impression that she was more than willing to listen and that she was ready to offer support and he found he had to curb an urge to tell her more. The notion of having someone like Hanna on his side was oddly compelling but Mac knew better than to let his guard down.

'I didn't know her,' he said. 'We were separated as infants. I didn't even know she existed until I was old enough to be allowed to make enquiries about who my biological parents were.'

'They separated twins? That's awful…'

Mac's breath came out in a soft huff. 'I think my adoptive parents were only interested in a boy. Someone to carry on the family name.'

'Did you manage to find your sister?'

Mac shook his head. 'No. She'd died several years before I found out about her, of a brain tumour.'

'Oh, no…' The sympathy in Hanna's tone was like a physical touch. 'That's so sad.'

'Not really.' Mac shrugged. 'As I said, I never knew her. We didn't even share a surname. Her name was Jenny Dalgliesh.'

'It still sounds Scottish.'

'Her parents were Scottish. They emigrated just after they adopted her. It did make me curious about how different our lives must have been. I thought that, maybe one day, I'd like to go and see what it was like in New Zealand.'

'You should,' Hanna told him, turning to walk on. 'You'd love it.' She threw him a sideways glance as he caught up with her. 'You know what's even more of a coincidence than me coming from where your sister grew up?'

'What's that?'

'I almost got adopted.'

'Almost?'

'My father had a passion for flying and both my parents were killed when his plane went down when I was young. My grandmother had no real interest in doing the child-raising thing again but, in the end, she decided she couldn't send me away.'

Mac looked at this confident, vivacious woman beside him, imagined how enchanting she might have been as a young girl and found himself smiling. 'It seems like it worked out pretty well.'

'Gran did her best,' Hanna agreed. 'But there were so many rules. And I wasn't that good at following them all.'

Mac laughed. He could imagine that, as well.

'The problem was that we didn't understand each other,' Hanna said. 'Like, I wanted to learn to dance but I got sent to ballet lessons. And then ballroom lessons. Not at all what I wanted.'

Mac shuddered. 'I had to do ballroom dancing lessons at boarding school.'

'Lots of rules. Not so much fun.'

'Is dancing ever *fun*?'

The flash in her eyes made them light up. 'Have you ever seen the movie *Dirty Dancing*?'

Mac shook his head, not because he had no idea what she was talking about but because his imagination was threatening to run away with him this time. He cleared his throat, needing to change the subject before his thoughts became entirely inappropriate considering he'd only just met this woman.

'This statue we're coming to is the one I was telling you about. The most famous on the Charles Bridge,' he told her. 'See those shiny parts of the brass plaques on the base of the statue? They've been polished by the thousands of hands that had touched it for luck.'

'Oh…' Hanna was well distracted. Or perhaps she was responding to his unspoken warning that their conversation had been getting too personal. 'You can never have too much luck, can you?' She joined a small queue, waiting to take her turn to touch the statue.

Mac stayed where he was, needing a moment to himself because he could feel a ripple of something that threatened to disturb the pleasure of Hanna's company and a new city to explore. He hadn't thought about how he'd felt to discover he'd had a sister in too many years to count but he could remember that pull that could have taken him to the other side of the world, just to see what it was like. He'd been well trained not to respond to the temptation of doing something when the consequences hadn't been considered enough, however. He'd known that responding to that kind of pull could lead to the kind of trouble that could make life a lot less bearable.

But here he was, with someone who had links to more than one aspect of his life—his work that he was so passionate about and to a buried part of his past that had shaped who he actually was to such a large extent. Someone who was becoming so increasingly captivating that Mac was actually tempted to let himself get pulled—a little way, at least—in whatever direction Hanna Peterson wanted to take him.

Good grief… Mac followed Hanna and stepped towards the statue of John of Nepomuk. He might have zero belief in unscientific concepts like superstition, but it might be prudent to touch this particular statue. Just to be on the safe side. Because it seemed like he could do with a bit of luck himself…

Hanna had been on plenty of guided tours in her years of travelling the globe but she'd never been on one quite like this.

Because this was Prague and it was an enchanted city.

Because her attraction to her guide had been there right from the start and it was steadily increasing as she noticed more and more about him. Like the way his eyes creased a little and made his gaze quite piercing as he focused on anything. It could have made him look suspicious, but his lips seemed to have a resting position of a faint smile so, instead, he looked as if he might be enjoying a private joke. His grooming— including his haircut—was immaculate. Hanna could imagine Mac wearing a tuxedo and looking as if he'd stepped straight out of a Bond movie from the leading role. His accent made her toes curl with delight to the extent that she was probably missing a lot of the information he was reading aloud from the guidebook, but it didn't matter.

Hanna was thoroughly enjoying herself.

They spent an hour exploring Prague Castle and it felt like they barely scratched the surface of the UNESCO monument.

'This is the largest continuous castle complex in the world,' Mac told her. 'It covers almost seventy thousand square metres.'

Hanna nodded solemnly. 'I think my feet are somehow already aware of this fact. They may be planning to stage a protest.'

'Do you want to stop?'

'*No...*' Her denial came out with slightly more emphasis than Hanna had intended but that was because the possibility had just occurred to her that when they stopped and parted ways, she might never see Mac again. And that prospect was...well, it was just something Hanna would prefer to put off for as long as she could.

'This is the best bit yet,' she added hastily, in case Mac could guess the main reason why she didn't want to stop. 'Look at that ceiling.'

She tilted her head back, relieved to escape catching Mac's gaze so she couldn't reveal *why* she didn't want to stop but she could feel his gaze resting on her face. Weirdly, it was making the skin on the rest of her body tingle. There was no doubt at all that there was some serious chemistry floating in the air between them. Hanna had to catch her breath as she found herself wondering what it might feel like if her skin was in contact with his. Or her lips…

'We could have a coffee soon,' Mac said. 'Or an early lunch? We passed some very nice-looking restaurants as we came off the Charles Bridge.'

They had. Restaurants with outdoor seating areas shaded by trees and umbrellas. Hanna had the feeling that Mac would choose one that also had linen tablecloths and polished silver cutlery and a wine list that he could peruse because he probably knew all about fine wines…

That summed him up completely, didn't it? He was a gentleman. Or the Scottish equivalent of high social ranking—a laird, perhaps? Whatever… A traditional class system was an alien concept to most New Zealanders and Hanna was beginning to wonder what it would be like to see Dr Hamish Mac-Millan unbuttoned a little.

She had a feeling she would like what was revealed very much indeed.

Oh, help… Hanna made herself focus on what she was staring at, high above them on the ceiling of this huge hall they were in. 'They've made the beams look like flowers,' she said. 'How gorgeous is that?'

'It's ribbed vaulting,' Mac said, consulting his book. 'Late Gothic style. Work started on Vladislav Hall in 1486 under the orders of the King of Bohemia and the hall was completed in 1502.'

'Bohemia,' Hanna murmured. 'No wonder I feel like this place is touching my soul.'

'You're boho?' Mac was grinning. 'Of course you are. I should have guessed from that floaty sort of top you're wearing. The strings with the tassels are a dead giveaway come to think of it.'

'There are way more important aspects than clothing to having any traits that might be seen as bohemian,' Hanna chided.

'Such as?'

'Being a wanderer. I've always loved to travel. To just arrive somewhere and follow my nose.'

'Really? You don't book tours? Or hotels?'

'Nope. It's not so much of an adventure if you know what's coming, is it?'

'I wouldn't know.' Mac was shaking his head. 'I've never tried it. What else?'

'Well, I'm a bit unconventional,' Hanna said obligingly. 'And I tend to like other people who don't slot into what might be considered "normal" boxes.'

'I'm super normal,' Mac said.

'No.' Hanna shook her head. 'I don't think so.'

Mac's eyebrows rose. 'What makes you say that?'

'I meet normal people every day. I've met countless thousands of them in my lifetime but...'

'But...?' He was giving her that piercing look again.

Hanna caught her lip between her teeth. Would it be a death knell to say the words that were on the tip of her tongue out loud? She gave herself a mental shove with the vague encouragement of fortune favouring the brave.

'But I've never met anyone quite like you,' she added softly.

He held her gaze for the longest time.

Long enough for Hanna's heart rate to pick up and even skip a beat. For that tingling sensation to sink well beneath skin level and take up residence deep in her belly where it found and instantly merged with the excitement that a new adventure always bestowed.

For a moment, she forgot the real reason she'd come to this beautiful European city. The conference where she hoped to learn so much and reconnect with the passion she had for her work seemed almost irrelevant— a mere background that was providing the opportunity of a meeting that felt significant enough to be potentially life-changing.

Which was ridiculous. For heaven's sake, she knew virtually nothing about this man, other than that he was a doctor who was going to be attending the same conference as herself and that he had a sister he'd never known who happened to live in Hanna's homeland. He could be the laird of a Scottish estate, for all she knew. He could well be married with half a dozen children. But it really did feel as if she was on the brink of something so big, it was almost scary. Okay, they clearly had very different personalities. He was so buttoned up and Hanna was open to almost anything but...well, everybody knew that opposites could attract.

And that made it easy to shrug off any significance. That was all this was. An attraction. The kind that was best suited to a brief period of time where it could erupt into flames instantly and burn itself out rapidly enough to not create anything more than a pleasant memory. Hanna Peterson didn't do significant. She really did have the soul of a wanderer and they always tended to be lone wolves, didn't they?

She had, however, had the pleasant experience of indulging in a holiday fling before now and, even if playing with the chemistry between them was as far as this went, it was still rather delicious.

'You know what?' she said to Mac.

'What?'

'I'm starving. Let's go and find some lunch.'

Perhaps he shouldn't have given Hanna the choice of where to eat but he'd expected that she'd choose one of those pleasant looking restaurants with their charming terraces, not a truck selling street food.

The glance she'd given him had made it

clear that this was some kind of test, however. She knew that he'd prefer to sit at a table and order something from a menu, didn't she? Was she pushing a boundary to see if she could put a label on what box to slot him into? If so, even though Mac wasn't sure why this was so important, she was going to be disappointed because he intended to pass this test with flying colours. He didn't want to be normal enough to be labelled.

He wanted Hanna to like him.

So he carried cardboard boxes of what was apparently a local specialty while Hanna searched for an acceptable place to stop and eat. He couldn't fault her choice, which was a low stone wall, under a tree, not far from a boat ramp advertising river cruises.

The food had an unpronounceable name and consisted of deep-fried cheese balls that came with salad, a bread roll and a small wooden fork. It was surprisingly delicious but alarmingly messy. When Mac bit through the crunchy, crumbed exterior of the ball, warm, gooey cheese dripped onto his fingers and would have ended up on his clothing if he hadn't immediately shifted it to arm's length.

Hanna laughed. 'You look like it's a bomb that's about to explode.'

'It's already trying to.'

'Try what I'm doing.' Hanna had torn open a section of her bread roll. She added salad and squashed a melty cheese ball into the middle.

Sure enough, it worked a treat, and it wasn't lost on Mac that if he'd been alone he might have discarded the food rather than end up with it all over his clothes and, if he had, he would have missed out on what ended up being the perfect lunch.

'This is heaven,' Hanna declared, happily, as she ate her last mouthful and wiped her fingers on a serviette. 'I'm officially in love with Prague.' She watched a river boat pulling up to moor at the jetty. 'Oh, look… I'm not the only one in love. There's a wedding party.'

They both watched as the group of people took their time disembarking as the bride and groom posed for photographs. Hanna was still smiling.

'I'll tell you a secret,' she said.

'What's that?'

'I'm here on honeymoon.'

Mac blinked. Surely that sensation suddenly filling his chest wasn't disappointment? *Envy*, even? Marriage was the last thing he'd ever want for himself, after all. He'd learned that lesson a very long time ago.

But there was a mischievous twinkle in Hanna's expression. 'Not my honeymoon,' she added. 'My friends'. And they did invite me along. Given that it's the closest I'll ever get to having one, I thought I'd try it out.'

That strange, unpleasant sensation escaped with his next breath.

'You're never going to have a honeymoon of your own?'

'I did say I was unconventional, didn't I? Marriage. Kids. Not for me.' Hanna was still watching the bride so Mac couldn't detect anything that might have undermined how genuine her statement was.

'We're on the same page there,' he said.

Hanna's sideways glance was curious. 'How old are you?'

'Forty-four.'

'And you've never been married?'

'Nope. I was engaged once,' Mac admitted. 'That was once too often.'

He could still see questions in her eyes, so he looked away to let her know it wasn't a subject he wanted to continue.

'Same,' he heard her say quietly. 'Guess we both dodged the marriage bullet.' She let her breath out in a sigh as she turned to watch the bride gathering her skirts to walk away. 'Pretty dress, though…'

Mac didn't say anything, distracted by a connection he could feel with Hanna that was so much deeper than their similar career choices. And spending time with her had also just become a lot safer than it might have otherwise felt.

'Fancy a cruise?' he asked. 'That wedding party is finished and it only takes forty-five minutes according to that sign.'

It didn't really matter if he didn't go through the conference registration process as soon as it opened, the way he normally would, did it? The desk would be open until this evening, after all, and there would be plenty of time to talk to his international colleagues over the next couple of days.

He'd thrown caution to the winds eating a meal he would never have chosen for himself, after all, and he'd thoroughly enjoyed it so who knew what he might be missing if he walked away from what was, in fact, the type of well-rehearsed tourist attraction he preferred? As a bonus, he would get a little more of Hanna's company before he had to focus on the professional reasons that had actually brought him to Prague.

A short time later, they were looping through the archways under the Charles Bridge and sailing slowly along the 'Devil's Channel', a canal with buildings crowding either side that was reminiscent of Venice. They listened to a commentary as they floated past historic buildings and got a wonderful view of the castle from a distance. Wearing the earplugs for the recorded information meant they weren't talking to each other but the way they kept sharing glances made it feel as if they were still communicating and that made it feel so very different from any other tourist tour that Mac had ever taken. If he was honest, he wasn't listening nearly as intently as he would have if he'd been alone and he probably completely missed all sorts of interesting facts about Prague's history.

And he didn't give a damn...

Hanna's feet were reminding her how far they'd walked by the time they were heading back to their hotel. Over the bridge again, through streets that were starting to look familiar and into the square where a new crowd was gathering in front of the famous clock, waiting for it to chime the hour.

'We never did get to see the apostles appear, did we?'

'We didn't,' Mac agreed. 'I seem to remember we were a bit preoccupied.'

'We've got time...' Hanna could see that Mac instantly recognised what had the potential to become a private joke. His eyes were doing that crinkly, focused thing again.

Hanna wasn't about to admit it, a couple of minutes later, but the windows sliding open and the brief parade of small figures appearing was a little underwhelming. She wouldn't have missed it, though, because it gave her an extra few minutes with Mac.

A complete stranger she'd just shared half a day with.

A man who, on surface appearances, could be her total opposite, and yet it felt like she could possibly be more than half in love with him already.

But it was time to say goodbye. She saw his glance shift to their hotel across the square and then drop to his watch. She could almost feel his withdrawal from being a carefree tourist who was happy to soak in the ambience of a fascinating new city to a professional who was here to attend an academic event.

There were hundreds of people attending this prestigious conference and it was quite likely that Hanna wasn't going to get another chance to talk to Mac, let alone spend any one-on-one time with him.

'It's been the best tour ever,' she told him. 'I really enjoyed it.'

'Me, too. I'm delighted to have met you, Hanna Peterson from Dunedin.'

'Thank you. I feel the same way, Hamish MacMillan, from not the raincoat clan in Scotland.'

They grinned at each other, and on impulse Hanna stood on tiptoes, put her arms around Mac's neck and kissed him.

Just a brief press of her lips against his but the effect was startling. Taken by surprise, Mac hadn't moved a muscle but it felt as if he'd just kissed her senseless because Hanna could feel her bones trying to melt.

Oops…

She caught his gaze for no more than a heartbeat, offering a quick smile to let him know it was no big deal. She kissed people goodbye all the time.

Then she turned to leave the clock in the same way she had arrived this morning.

At a run.

CHAPTER THREE

IT WAS LATE that evening that Hanna remembered the shoelace.

Not that Jo had mentioned it, when they'd met up late this afternoon to register for the conference and then find a quiet table at one of the outdoor restaurants in the Old Town Square to have dinner together, but what if Jo wanted to go for a walk tomorrow when she needed a break from the conference programme and couldn't wear her comfortable shoes because Hanna still had her shoelace?

She'd be asleep by now and Hanna had no intention of disturbing the newlyweds but she put the lace into an envelope and walked quietly along the hotel corridor, hoping no one would see her. She'd been getting ready for bed herself when she'd remembered the borrowed item and was wearing only leggings and a sweatshirt over her camisole.

Her face was scrubbed free of makeup, her feet were bare and her hair hung in a rough braid down her back.

It was easy enough to slip the envelope under Cade and Jo's door and Hanna headed back to her own room. She ignored the doors to one of the lifts sliding open as she went past until she heard what sounded like her own name. And then she froze. She knew that voice.

That accent…

Oh, help… Hanna knew, even before she turned, that Mac would still be more than acceptably dressed for appearing in public and that his hair would look as if it had been combed very recently. If she'd wanted to accentuate how different they were from each other or confirm his opinion that any leanings towards being Bohemian meant dressing like a misplaced hippie, she couldn't have done a better job, could she? Good grief, her sweatshirt featured a peace sign made up of colourful flowers and, for heaven's sake, she had a tiny, braided silver toe ring on.

Mac had already noticed that toe ring, dammit. Or was he caught by the fact that Hanna was wandering the hotel corridors barefoot and braless? There was certainly something she hadn't seen before simmering in those dark, dark eyes.

'You're still up?'

The question was rhetorical but Hanna nodded as if it required an answer. Then she smiled. 'So are you.'

'I had an invitation to a cocktail party that went on rather a long time.' Mac held up a bottle he was holding as if it was part of his explanation. 'I tasted a champagne that was so good, I bought a bottle.' One of his eyebrows quirked. 'Maybe you'd like to try it?'

He was giving her that scrunchy eyed intense gaze again and Hanna could feel it all the way to that toe ring. She could feel herself swallow rather carefully because she knew exactly where this was heading. This was pretty much a textbook beginning to a holiday fling and this was the moment that Hanna had a choice.

Except it didn't feel like she did have a choice because the attraction that had been there between them since early this morning had flames licking its edges and it would only take a breath of oxygen in the right place to have it explode into an inferno. But it would be all the better for having that breath held for as long as possible.

So Hanna simply tilted her head as if she was giving the invitation careful thought.

'I do like champagne,' she said.

What on earth did he think he was doing?

There was only one reason that you invited a woman into your hotel room at this time of night. It wasn't the first time Mac had gone down this track but it was most definitely the first time with someone he'd only met a matter of hours ago.

Maybe that toe ring had tipped the balance and made him lose any common sense. Or maybe it was that Hanna Peterson was simply becoming increasingly intriguing.

Or perhaps it was as simple as knowing that he wanted this woman. A desire as old as time for a single male instinctively searching for a mate that had hit him like a brick earlier today when Hanna had brushed her lips against his in farewell. Or was it just a human need for a connection he hadn't had for too long?

Whatever... He wasn't about to make a move on Hanna. Not this soon. He just couldn't resist the chance to be near her again. To let this feeling of desire fizz through his veins and make him feel more alive than he had in a very long time.

They drank the champagne, sitting out on his balcony, listening to the chimes in the square strike eleven o'clock.

'Did you ask for this room specially so you could sit out here and see your clock?'

'No. It was an unexpected bonus.' Mac raised his glass. 'Like meeting you.'

'I had the best time on our tour,' Hanna agreed.

'Me, too.' Mac couldn't look away from her. He loved the way those tiny curls of hair were escaping that long braid to frame her face and the way her skin looked almost pearlescent in the soft light from a streetlamp below. His mouth tilted on one side. 'Time seems to be a bit of a theme for us, doesn't it?'

'Everybody needs reminding sometimes that time can be short,' Hanna said. 'And that it's important to make the most of it. Especially when you're only going to be somewhere for a day or two.'

Oh…man… Was Hanna taking the first step to making this happen? Was she offering him a night he could be quite sure he was never going to forget? He'd always been quite sure he was immune to being seduced. That he could always stay completely in control at all times. It seemed that that assumption might be incorrect.

And, in this moment, Mac couldn't have cared less.

But he could see a flash of what looked like vulnerability in those amazing eyes. Because Hanna was offering an invitation that might be rejected?

As if...

He could take at least an element of control back, couldn't he? And let her rest assured that her invitation was more than welcome. Mac got to his feet. He only needed to hold out his hands for Hanna to take them and it took only the tiniest tug for her to be on her feet and then in his arms. It didn't really matter who initiated that kiss because it seemed they both wanted it just as much as each other. As Hanna's lips parted beneath his and he felt the exquisite touch of her tongue against his, Mac gave up overthinking any of this.

There were no rules.

Time was indeed short and they should both absolutely make the most of it.

Walking into the hotel dining room the next morning, Hanna quickly spotted the table where Jo and Cade were sitting near a window. By the time she joined them, with a cup of strong coffee in her hands, the chimes in the square had finished announcing that it was eight o'clock. In an hour, the conference would be opened by a welcome speech in the main hall before the attendees would splinter into groups for the first of many presentations and workshops spread over the entire conference facilities.

'Morning.' Hanna took the empty seat beside Jo. She looked at the breakfast Cade had chosen of muesli with yoghurt and fruit and then at the plate in front of Jo that had a pastry stuffed full of what looked like custard. 'Mmm…healthy,' she murmured. 'What is that? A cronut?'

'I'm not sure.' Jo grinned. 'But it's delicious. And the pregnant lady gets to eat whatever she wants for breakfast.' She was about to take another bite but took another glance at Hanna instead.

'You look…different,' she said.

'Oh…?' Hanna closed her eyes, taking a sip of her excellent coffee. She needed it. She suspected she might look different because she'd had almost no sleep last night.

Thanks to Hamish MacMillan.

Or maybe it was thanks to the Gods of Holiday Flings. Or the sheer luck of bumping into Mac when she'd left her room, late last evening, on her way back from returning the forgotten shoelace.

'Maybe it's your hair.' Jo was still staring at Hanna when she opened her eyes again. 'You don't usually braid it like that, do you?'

'No.' Hanna had put braids along the side of her head as well as in the length of her hair. 'It needed taming.'

Because it had been such a mission to get all the knots out this morning that it had made her long hair extra wildly wavy. The pain of combing out every tangle had been worth it, though. Hanna had to push away the memories of Mac pulling the tie from the bottom of her loose braid and raking it loose with his fingers so that its length tickled her naked back as he held her head and kissed her until her bones really did melt. Or had she been kissing him? There was no getting away from the fact that she'd been the one to blow on those flames in the first place and create the wildfire.

'Hmm…' Jo took a bite of her pastry and her words were muffled. 'Suits you.'

'Is that a spare seat by any chance?'

The voice with its lilt of a Scottish accent came from right behind Hanna. Luckily, she'd already put her coffee cup back onto its saucer so nothing got spilt. She sent out a silent plea to the universe that nobody would be able to guess the effect that Mac's voice was having on her body. That ripple felt like an aftershock of the most amazing sex she'd ever experienced in her life.

'Yes. Please…join us.' Cade pushed his chair back.

'Don't get up.' Mac set a plate of scrambled eggs and bacon onto the table. 'Good morning, Hanna. How are you?'

Hanna wasn't sure she was quite brave enough to make eye contact with Mac. A mere glance at the rest of his body was doing odd things to her heart rate. He was wearing an immaculate pinstriped suit that included a waistcoat. So very formal. He was buttoned up again, but Hanna knew the astonishing flipside of that coin now, didn't she? Could she even bring herself to say anything to him or was a sudden embarrassment stealing her voice? Had she been testing herself or Mac last night, being more adventurous than she'd ever been in bed before?

Wild. That was the only word for the sex

they'd shared. And how amazing was it that Mac had gone along with every move? Not that they'd swung from the chandeliers, exactly, but...oh, *my*...

It was Jo who spoke quickly enough for any hesitation from Hanna to be disguised.

'You two know each other?' Her sideways glance was eloquent. Hanna hadn't said anything about how attractive her companion had been.

'We met yesterday.' Mac nodded. He was unwrapping his cutlery. As cool as a cucumber. Nobody would ever, ever guess just how well they now knew each other.

'Really?' Cade also sounded surprised.

'I told you during dinner last night.' To her relief, Hanna's voice sounded perfectly normal. 'I had the pleasure of Mac's company to explore Prague, after my walking tour didn't happen.'

'Ah, I remember...' Cade mirrored Mac's nod. 'The tour guide who gave you such an appropriate introduction to the conference by providing an emergency situation on our doorstep.'

'This is Hamish MacMillan,' Hanna said. 'Mac, these are my friends, Cade and Jo. Jo's an emergency medicine specialist from the hospital I work in and Cade is a critical care paramedic.'

Mac smiled across the table at Jo and shook hands with Cade. 'You've all come a long way to attend this conference.' He turned to Jo. 'The trip can't have been easy for you.'

'My feet are a bit puffy still,' Jo admitted. 'But I had to come. Cade's presenting a paper about the pre-hospital use of CPAP.' Her pride in her husband was obvious. 'And it's our honeymoon.'

'Oh…congratulations.' Mac shot a glance at Hanna and she grinned back at him.

Hanna knew that he was remembering their conversation yesterday when she'd told him she was sharing her friends' honeymoon, but she could see beneath that layer as well, to where he was also thinking about what had happened in his room last night. It wasn't so easy for him to appear in such control of his facial features, after all, was it?

'Hanna was our bridesmaid when we got married last week,' Jo told him. She grinned. 'It seemed a bit rude not to invite her to join our honeymoon.'

'We are having some time to ourselves after the conference,' Cade added. 'Just a couple of days for me and Jo, sadly, but we need to get home well before the new addition to our family thinks it might be a good idea to make an entrance. Hanna's the lucky one—she gets to float around Europe for another couple of weeks at least.'

'Where are you based, Mac?' Jo asked. 'I think Hanna said something about New York?'

'You mentioned you were in Central Park recently,' Hanna said. To her relief, it was not as hard as she expected to keep sounding completely casual. 'I might have made an assumption.'

'Not an entirely incorrect one,' Mac admitted, around mouthfuls of his breakfast. 'I have been living in New York for the last eighteen months. I had a fellowship at a research institute attached to a hospital with an excellent emergency department while I was working on a PhD.'

'And that's completed? Congratulations.' Jo's tone was impressed. 'I know how much work that is.'

'I completed it a little faster than expected,' Mac said. 'Which is why I'm currently unemployed.'

Hanna's eyes widened. Partly because of

Mac's surprising comment, but also because his foot was touching hers under the table. Even if it wasn't deliberate, it was sending another one of those aftershocks rippling through her body. She wasn't avoiding eye contact this time, however. She was waiting for him to look up so she could see if he might be as aware of that touch as she was.

But Mac seemed to be trying to fit exactly the right combination of eggs and bacon onto a very small square of toast, so Hanna was left to remember not only the way he'd licked drippy cheese off his fingers yesterday but the touch of his tongue on parts of her body that had been the most extraordinary sensual experience ever.

'I took two years' leave from my position at an Edinburgh hospital,' Mac continued. 'Which means I might need to find an adventure or two to keep me out of mischief for a while.'

His foot moved against Hanna's. Deliberately. Her breath left her body in a long sigh. A quiet sigh, but Mac had heard it, judging by the flick of a glance that grazed her own. The way the lines around his mouth deepened made her wonder if he was suppressing a smile.

'Well...' Cade was grinning at Mac. 'If you get desperate, I know of a locum position in New Zealand that's going begging. Jo needs cover for the maternity leave that I hope she's going to start very soon.'

Mac's huff of laughter sounded no more than a polite acknowledgement that he'd heard the suggestion. He shifted his foot away from Hanna's, ate the last mouthful of his breakfast and got to his feet. 'If you'll excuse me,' he said, 'I have a bit of preparation to do before the programme starts. It's been a pleasure to meet you. I hope we get the chance to talk more later.' His gaze rested a moment on Hanna and, while he didn't say anything aloud, she got the distinct impression that he intended to do more than simply talk to *her* later.

She could feel her toes curling inside her shoes.

She was rather hoping that might happen herself.

'Nice guy,' Cade said, watching Mac stride across the dining room. 'Shame he isn't keen on the idea of a locum in New Zealand.'

Hanna couldn't see Mac sitting anywhere amongst the crowd gathering for the opening address of this conference but that was hardly surprising. There were hundreds of attendees packed into this auditorium. Jo's obviously advanced pregnancy had people scrambling to find them the best seats, however, and they settled in as a conference organiser welcomed them and attended to administrative information such as fire exits, bathroom facilities and where to access details on the scientific programme available. Then he turned to introducing the speaker who was going to open this conference.

'This man will be no stranger to a great many people here, with his more than three hundred published papers and numerous engagements to speak at international conferences. As a recipient of awards that recognise and celebrate innovative and extraordinary work by healthcare individuals and teams in the field of emergency medicine and having just come from a limited tenure as a director of a research collaboration in the United States, it's my pleasure to welcome Dr Hamish MacMillan.'

Hanna's jaw dropped. She barely felt the nudge from Jo's elbow or heard her soft exclamation because she was watching Mac walk across the stage to stop in front of the lectern. He was silent for a moment, looking out at his audience, and even from a distance, Hanna knew it was that focused look that deepened the tiny lines at the corners of his eyes. She was still so stunned by the fact that she had spent most of yesterday playing with possibly the most eminent conference attendee here that she barely listened to him congratulating the conference organisers on the wide-ranging topics being presented over the next two days. She wasn't watching the images appearing on the screen behind Mac, either. She was simply watching him, so aware of how intimately she now knew this man. It was a real effort to tune into what he was saying.

'Adversity, like necessity, can inspire invention or advances that can accelerate changes likely to benefit us all. The challenges we've all faced in recent times, dealing with a global pandemic, has given us a new perspective on the big picture areas like the management systems and surge capacities of our hospitals and emergency departments. Advances in technology are becoming a beneficial part of the "new normal" but cyber-attacks are a very real threat.

Like all of you, I'm looking forward to hearing about the latest advances and innovations but I'd like to finish my welcome by a reminder that—like the pixels in a digital image—the big picture is made up of a great many small pictures. And I'd like to leave you, this morning, with the example of one of those small pictures.'

The screen went dark behind Mac. The lights in the auditorium seemed to soften and there was a long pause before Mac started speaking in a very different tone. His voice was quieter. Compelling. Hanna could feel a tingle that had nothing to do with what she and Mac had been doing in the hours before dawn. She suspected that everyone in this vast room was as captivated as she was by what Mac was about to say. He had his entire audience in the palm of his hand as he began to talk about a four-year-old boy who was sitting in a cubicle in an emergency department. Mac was as much in control of what was happening in this auditorium as he had been yesterday, directing a crowd and taking over the management of a medical situation in a public square.

'So his mother says that the wee lad got a new bike for his birthday and he's taken a tumble while learning to use it without his trainer wheels. You hear the unspoken message that this is a family that cares enough about their child to give him a brand-new bike. The mother's not trying to comfort the boy but she's tough. Working class. Old school. It's not as if this hasn't happened before. The child is clearly accident prone, isn't he? And maybe the lad's not saying anything, but an ED is a scary place for any child, isn't it?'

Hanna wasn't missing anything Mac was saying now. She could see that little boy, sitting on a bed behind the curtain of a cubicle. Maybe his mother was sitting on the chair beside the bed. As nervous as her son?

'You're busy,' Mac continued. 'Your department is stretched to almost breaking point. There's a major trauma in Resus One and multiple victims from a pile-up on the motorway are on their way in with an ETA of less than five minutes. Have you currently got the resources to cope? Could you be on the brink of a Code Black where you're beyond capacity enough to affect patient care? Okay, so this kid has bruises in places you might not expect to find them. Like on his ears and the angle of that small jaw. But look at how happy he is to get picked up by the nurse and carried off to get an X-ray on that probable arm fracture. You're happy, too. You can get back to the big picture of keeping your department functioning within acceptable parameters.'

Hanna was holding her breath. She knew what wasn't being said here because she'd had training in recognising non-accidental injuries in children who were the victims of abuse. She'd seen cases herself that would haunt her for ever and she could actually feel the prickle of tears behind her eyes.

Another tone-change in Mac's voice as he continued speaking sent a shiver down Hanna's spine. He was passionate about this. She felt like she was getting a glimpse into the soul of a dedicated and compassionate physician. A person she could have the utmost respect for.

'Think about this,' Mac said softly. 'What if that wee lad—that tiny pixel in the grand image—might be happy to go with that nurse because your emergency department is becoming his safe space? Perhaps it's the only space where it feels like someone cares about him. It might not be as dramatic or have the instant results of cracking a chest in Resus but it's quite possible that paying more attention to that tiny picture can also save a life.'

Hanna only let out that breath she was holding as Mac finished his speech by more words of welcome and his prediction that the next two days would be inspirational, motivational and a very real pleasure for everybody lucky enough to be here.

He'd hit that nail on the head, she decided. Hanna was feeling incredibly lucky to be here. Lucky to have spent time with the most astonishing man she'd ever met. And it was lucky she hadn't known exactly who he was when she had met him. It was unthinkable that she'd told an international rock star of emergency medicine that he wasn't at all normal and it was almost appalling in retrospect that she'd practically offered to jump into bed with him without waiting for an invitation.

But there it was. It had happened and, judging by that look on Mac's face as he'd left their breakfast table, it might well happen again.

Yeah…she was very, very lucky…

CHAPTER FOUR

THE FIRST FULL day of the conference programme passed in something of a blur for Mac, who was in high demand to participate in discussion panels and sought after for conversations regarding his research work or for networking amongst a large group of people who were passionate about their careers.

He managed to slip into a spare seat at the back of a small lecture theatre where Hanna's friend Cade was presenting his seminar on CPAP—Continuous Positive Airway Pressure—a ventilation technique that was well proven to be beneficial in a wide variety of clinical situations ranging from acute heart failure and respiratory failure from viral causes to the inhalation of toxic fumes or simply a complication from morbid obesity. From the viewpoint of prehospital medical care, he was on a mission for the single-use, disposable devices to be adopted as standard operating procedures in every emergency medical service because anything less had become a failure in duty of care.

Cade was undoubtedly preaching to the converted here, but he was an engaging, confident presenter and had clear and effective diagrams and graphs to back up his position and statistics. Like Mac had done himself this morning in his welcoming speech, Cade used a case history that gave a personal touch to what could be merely clinical data. The paper deserved to be published and could make a difference by reaching a much greater audience that way. Mac knew he had to move on swiftly to his next highlighted slots on the programme, so he got to his feet, ready to leave the room, as soon as the applause for Cade's presentation began. Someone else also jumped up in the front row of seating. Someone who was holding her hands a little higher and clapping a little louder than other people. She was also beaming with pride and Mac found himself smiling as he left the room. It wasn't any surprise that Hanna's congratulations for her friend were as enthusiastic as the way she approached many things in her life.

Including sex…

Good grief… Mac had never experienced a night quite like last night in his entire life. The way Hanna could simply be in the moment and both give and receive a physical pleasure with what seemed like no limits had been more than the most satisfying sexual experience Mac had ever had. There had been a joy to be found in even something as fleeting as an unexpected few hours in bed with someone you might never see again in your life. A memory that Mac suspected would be able to bestow an echo of that joy whenever he chose to let it surface in the future.

For now, however, it needed to be tucked away where it belonged. Maybe it would be a good thing if he didn't see Hanna again because he might need to find a very secure mental space to ensure he didn't get completely distracted from the job he was here to do.

His next commitment was to join a discussion on emerging vulnerabilities in emergency care, like high consequence infectious diseases that, as they had all learned only too well recently, carried the risk of crippling even the most highly regarded health care systems. He could relax a little after that, perhaps, with what should be an enjoyable extended session as he facilitated a disaster management workshop for a limited number of attendees, but he would still need to be focused. Mac had never let anything personal interfere with how he did his job and he wasn't about to start now.

'I'm so excited about this workshop.'

'Me, too.' Cade was leading the way to the last session of the day that Hanna was also registered for. 'It'll be great to do something hands-on after listening to so many presentations today.'

'Are you enjoying the programme?'

'Absolutely. I just went to a panel discussion on advances in PPE, which was very useful. You?'

'The best one so far was a presentation on closing wounds on old, fragile skin. That's something I do all the time and sometimes you end up making things worse but there's these new dermal clips that are not only fast and effective but virtually painless.' Hanna beamed at Cade. 'I'm inspired. When I get home, I'm going to make it my mission to have them available.' Hanna stopped at the door of a seminar room. 'How's this going to work? I can't see anything set up for a disaster management scenario.'

'I heard someone say that there's a bus. Sounds like we get taken somewhere else after the introduction.'

'Oh…wow… I can't wait.'

Hanna followed him into the room that already had its lights dimmed in preparation for a multimedia presentation. Maybe that was why she didn't notice who one of the people standing behind the lectern was. Until he started speaking, anyway.

Until that irresistible accent was making her skin tingle and she could barely focus on what was being said about the content of this session and how it would run. Who knew that the famous Dr Hamish MacMillan was also an expert in an emergency medical response to a multi-casualty disaster?

She'd managed, by and large, to not let him intrude on her thoughts as she'd navigated back-to-back, attention-grabbing presentations but even the excitement of feeling inspired by something new, like those dermal clips, was only a distant hum as she tuned in to what Mac was actually saying instead of being totally distracted by a visceral reaction to his presence.

'A disaster is any event that overwhelms the available resources. It can be natural, accidental or intentional. We're talking earthquakes, tsunamis, hurricanes. A fire in a multi-storey apartment block, perhaps. A plane crash or train derailment. Or a mass shooting or detonation of an explosive device in a crowded space. Unfortunately, we see far too many examples of these kinds of disasters and no country or community is immune.'

There were images appearing behind Mac, as a backdrop. The kind of images that they had all seen on international news broadcasts—a silent portrayal of the human suffering in the immediate aftermath of a catastrophic event. People covered in dust streaked with blood, stumbling to safety amidst collapsed buildings or other carnage or trying to help those who were unable to move. By the time the screen changed to outline the response they were going to practise today, everyone in the room was intently focused on what Mac was outlining. It didn't matter how many times they might have heard it before, this felt different, and

Hanna had no doubt that it was because of the charisma of the man who was speaking.

A charisma that had drawn her in far enough during their first meeting to make her realise how easy it would be to fall for him. And that was before she'd listened to his opening address this morning and she'd heard someone who was internationally respected in his field, capable of running an entire emergency department, focus his attention on a single child who might get lost in the system. The idea that he could zoom in on the kaleidoscope of his professional arena and care about a small boy who might be a victim of abuse had pulled Hanna even further down that track and that was entirely separate from knowing how skilled he was as a lover.

Oh, my…

Hamish MacMillan might well be the perfect man. He was probably setting a bar far too high for anyone else to ever compete with but why would that matter when Hanna had pretty much given up on finding a life partner anyway?

'You're going to be taken to an abandoned warehouse complex, which isn't far away. Our colleagues here in Prague have staged a simulation of a bomb blast and we have approximately fifty local volunteers who are acting as patients for us in two separate locations.'

Hanna caught Cade's gaze as her jaw dropped. This was far more than she had been expecting and she was suddenly nervous.

'You will each have a kit with minimal equipment—triage tags, oral airways and tourniquets—and you will have a limited time to individually triage and record your findings and decisions. When that time is up, whether or not you are finished, you will have to stop so the scene will be reset for the next person. One of the session leaders will accompany you to answer your questions in English and provide clinical data when appropriate. They will also discuss your results with you afterwards.'

Any hope that she might have been able to partner with Cade for the exercise vanished. Hanna could only hope she wasn't about to make a complete fool of herself in front of Mac. She wasn't the only person who was listening intently as Mac swiftly covered the basics of the START triage system they would be following.

'Simple Triage and Rapid Transport. I'm sure you're all familiar with the principle, which is to swiftly identify issues that could be fatal within an hour—breathing problems, head injuries and significant bleeding.'

For an intense thirty minutes Mac made the process look simple.

'Clear any minor injuries or green labels from the scene. If people can understand directions and can move to a designated area without assistance, they are unlikely to die soon. Those that are left, unless there are hearing or language issues, are those injured too badly to move, or they are unconscious or dead and these patients are your priorities.'

There were specific instructions to be followed. If a patient wasn't breathing you could reposition them to open their airway, but if they didn't start breathing spontaneously you had to assume they were dead and move on immediately. Red tags to designate critical condition were given to people including those who had a respiration rate greater than thirty a minute or less than ten, no palpable radial pulse or with a lowered level of consciousness.

Hanna's head was spinning as she tried to lock every instruction into her brain. It didn't help that she could feel Mac watching her as she followed the group to where a bus was waiting outside. This was the kind of challenge she'd always loved in her training, but it had never felt quite this important to perform at her absolute best. She wanted Mac to notice her, of course she did—but preferably for reasons she could be proud of.

For some unknown reason, Mac had been quite confident that Hanna would not be at any of the conference sessions he was involved with. Perhaps he had seen his interaction with her as simply part of his personal life and therefore quite separate from anything professional? Had making that distinction made it more acceptable to have told her things he wouldn't have dreamed of saying to a colleague? Had it also made acceptable something he would never have dreamed of doing normally—like taking a woman he'd only just met to his bed?

Having even an imaginary boundary between personal and professional blurred to this extent was disturbing and the only defence mechanism that Mac could come up with on the spot was to focus more fiercely on the professional aspect of this unexpected encounter. Maybe that was why he found himself pushing Hanna harder than any of the other workshop attendees when he found he was the session leader to accompany her run through the scenario.

He'd already seen more than one person completely fazed by the horribly realistic scenario his Czech colleagues had put together. Would Hanna also get caught in the headlights and miss the first—and possibly most important—step of the triage process?

Apparently not.

She stopped for a long moment in the doorway of this space that had groaning bodies lying on the floor, people stumbling around amongst upturned furniture and broken building materials. There was background noise of some machinery and a smoke machine was adding to the atmosphere. Several of the volunteer victims were calling for help and the last workshop attendee to come in for their run had immediately gone towards the loudest of them.

Not Hanna. She took a long, sweeping gaze around this big space.

'Is the scene safe?'

'Yes,' Mac confirmed.

She put the tip of her thumb and forefinger into her mouth and let out a whistle that could have been effective in bringing sheep-dogs back from the far corners of a large paddock. It startled everybody—volunteers, helpers and Mac—enough for the noise to diminish instantly.

'Could everybody who can walk please come over here?' Hanna called, her voice loud and clear. 'Stay in this corner until somebody comes to see you.'

And, just like that, the scene became more manageable as at least ten people removed themselves. Hanna could now start her run, knowing that she wouldn't be wasting time on patients that weren't critical.

Mac followed her. He wasn't about to let her know how impressed he already was, which was just as well as he only became more impressed within the next minutes.

Victim number One was unresponsive and Hanna immediately tilted his head back to open his airway.

'No spontaneous breaths,' Mac told her.

Hanna gave a single nod, put a black label on the victim and moved on only seconds after she'd arrived. Victim number Two was groaning. The moulage to present the look of an injury had been excellent and this per-son appeared to have his femur protruding through the skin of his thigh. The artists had also been generous with the fake blood.

Hanna felt for a radial pulse.

'No radial pulse,' Mac said instantly.

'Respiration rate?'

'Twenty-eight.'

'Do I see active bleeding from the open fracture?'

'Yes. Active, pulsatile bleeding.'

Hanna opened her kit, pulled out a tourniquet and slipped it around the top of the man's leg. She fed the end of the strap through the buckle but only tightened it a little and didn't twist the rod.

'Bleeding has stopped.' Mac nodded.

'I'll be back as soon as I can.' Hanna smiled at her patient as she gave him a red, immediate attention required label. 'I promise…'

She was already on her way, actually running to cover the space between this person and the next in the shortest time possible. Mac followed, noting the smile on the face of the volunteer and the thumbs-up signal that Hanna had missed. This might only be pretence, but he had appreciated the reassurance and, if this scenario was real, that could have made all the difference to someone who was in severe pain and terrified.

She dealt with another half a dozen patients just as efficiently. Someone who was sitting, holding their head but apparently too dizzy to walk, received a yellow, priority two label. The person who was loudly calling for help and crying with pain, who had a fracture/dislocation of their elbow, was encouraged to get to their feet and join the other mobile patients in the green category.

Hanna got through the whole scenario in less time than the doctors Mac had previously accompanied, and her triage labelling had been faultless, but he wanted to push her further.

'Why did you re-categorise patient number eight who had no visible injuries from the bomb blast and a good radial pulse?'

'Because he didn't make it to the green category area. He had to sit down due to chest pain and needed to be seen soon so that a heart attack could be ruled out so I changed him from green to yellow.'

'And the woman with the baby who had been able to walk? Why did you change her?'

'Because of the baby. Any child under twelve months old is automatically a priority one and needs a red label, don't they?'

Mac had another half a dozen questions

on the tip of his tongue but found himself shaking his head as he smiled.

'You've done this before, haven't you?'

Hanna also shook her head. 'I've had some training in triage but I've never done a scenario like this.' Her face lit up. 'It was brilliant.'

'*You* were brilliant,' Mac finally had to tell her. 'I'd have you on my response team anytime.' And, just like that, the boundary between professional and personal evaporated.

'I'm in,' Hanna said. 'After this, I'll have far more confidence if I ever have to do it for real. I'm so glad I came.'

So was Mac. He was still holding Hanna's gaze. Until someone called from the other side of the space.

'Reset completed. We're ready to go again.'

'No rest for the wicked.' He smiled. 'Maybe I'll see you again tonight at the conference dinner?'

The volunteers were in place and had started their groaning and calling as Hanna turned to leave. The smoke machine was puffing out another, realistic addition to a post-explosion scenario. And Hanna smiled back.

'See you there.'

* * *

The glow of having Dr Hamish MacMillan tell her that she had met the challenge of the disaster response scenario so well—that she was *brilliant*, in fact—was still with Hanna as she arrived for the gala dinner that evening, having paid somewhat more attention to her attire and makeup than usual. When she saw Mac, at the centre of a group across the elegant venue that was part of Prague Castle itself, that glow got ramped up to a heat that had the potential to melt her bones.

'Ooh…' Jo was right beside Hanna. 'That's your personal tour guide over there, isn't it?'

'Mmm…'

She couldn't look away. Mac had been gorgeous in his crisp, white shirt and chinos yesterday, immaculately professional in the suit he'd been wearing this morning but dressed up in a formal, black-tie outfit, he looked more than ever like the hero of a Bond movie.

He also looked as if he was excusing himself from the group of people around him. Hanna watched him make a beeline for one of the waiters balancing flutes of champagne on silver platters, but she only realised he had spotted her entrance when he turned to come in her direction, holding the two glasses he had picked up. People were turning to see who had caught his attention and Hanna felt suddenly, uncharacteristically, shy. Thank goodness she hadn't known how famous Mac was when she'd first met him.

She took a steadying breath as she accepted the glass he offered. 'How did you guess I like champagne?'

'Everybody likes champagne, don't they?'

It looked as if it had taken an effort for Mac to drag his gaze away from hers. To not sink into the reminder of what the offer of champagne had led to last night. He turned towards Jo.

'I'm so sorry. I would have brought you a glass as well but there didn't seem to be a non-alcoholic option.'

'No worries. Cade's gone to find me a sparkling water,' Jo said. She seemed to be fighting an urge to smile as she shifted her gaze to Hanna. 'I might just go and see where he's got to.'

'Did I chase her away?' Mac dipped his head so that he could lower his voice and still be heard. 'I'd say "sorry" but...' His voice was a low growl now. 'But I'm not really sorry. I much prefer to have you all to myself.'

Okay… Hanna was definitely melting now. She struggled to find something coherent to say. 'I had no idea you're so famous,' she confessed. 'I had a bit of a cheek expecting you to become a private tour guide, didn't I?'

'It could become my new hobby,' Mac said. 'Perhaps I should take notes on how the professionals do it this week. I'm booked on a tour across Germany.'

'Oh? Apart from a visit to Berlin a long time ago, I've never spent much time in Germany.'

'Neither have I. I chose this tour because it was an exact fit for the time I have available and it starts right here in Prague. I can miss the first day tomorrow but join the group in the evening. On Monday, we head to Lauf, in Bavaria and then it's Würzburg, Frankfurt and numerous other highlights before the trip ends in Amsterdam. From there I can fly straight to a conference in Paris where I'm presenting some of my research results.'

With a national reputation for less than flexible organisation, Germany was still not on Hanna's radar as a preferred destination. She could imagine Mac enjoying it, however.

'I'm heading off tomorrow as well,' she told him.

'Where to?'

'I have no idea. I'll get onto one of those "last minute" or "grab-a-seat" websites and see what's available. Or I might just head for the train station or the airport and see what fate has in store for me.'

Mac nodded. 'I remember you saying that you liked to follow your nose rather than booking things.'

'Because you find the best adventures that way,' Hanna agreed.

'That sounds like a more exciting hobby than being a tour guide.'

'This trip is certainly proving memorable so far.' Hanna took a rather large gulp of her drink. 'Perhaps I should consider making holiday flings *my* new hobby?'

Mac blinked. The commendable speed with which he caught up on her train of thought was unsurprising in someone of his intelligence, but his next words took Hanna completely by surprise.

'It might be possible to combine our new

hobbies,' he said. 'In order to test whether they are worth pursuing?'

Hanna's gaze was fixed on his, her eyebrows lifting in a silent query.

'I have double rooms booked for my tour across Germany and I happen to know that there is an empty seat on the bus beside me. I'm sure I could arrange a ticket for you. Entirely my treat. And, if we're both doing something new, that could also be an adventure, yes?'

'But what would be new for you?' Hanna asked. 'Apart from getting tips on being a tour guide?'

'Having my first "holiday fling",' Mac told her. His slight hesitation was telling. 'Having company...'

Oh...

Was having company an unusual thing for him? Did Dr Hamish MacMillan, internationally acclaimed emergency specialist and sought-after conference speaker, have a gap in his personal life that meant he was lonely?

The fleeting image of a small boy transfixed in front of a television screen, those dark eyes as big as saucers as he soaked in technical information about an historical clock because he'd fallen in love with its complexity reminded Hanna that this man had already captured a little part of her heart.

The poignant tug on her heartstrings at the idea that he might be lonely, even if it was a personal choice, for whatever reason, to be single had just captured an even larger part of her heart. This might not be wise, but it was definitely irresistible.

Hanna drained her glass of champagne as a waiter went past. She put her empty glass on his tray. She met Mac's gaze over the rim of the full glass she had exchanged it for and it looked as though she was taking a deep breath at the same time.

'Okay,' she said. 'I'm in.'

CHAPTER FIVE

HANNA CAME CLOSE to changing her mind about the bus trip through Germany when she arrived at the meeting place to catch the bus on Monday morning and found a young German tour guide, glaring at her.

'This is most unusual.' According to her name badge, the guide was called Katarina. 'To have one person join a tour a day late is unsettling for everybody else. But...*two* people? One who is not even on my manifest?'

Hanna eyed the queue of people outside this hotel, who were waiting to board the bus. They looked as if they had a lot in common with each other, and having had a day to explore Prague they gave the impression they had clearly bonded as a group intending to have a wonderful holiday together. They were all at least a generation older than herself. Some looked old enough to be her grandparents and she could tell that her jeans with their frayed cuffs and her smocked top were being deemed to be on the scruffy side. She caught the moment they relaxed a little and, to her amusement, found that it was because Mac had arrived. Looking as tidy as ever and totally responsible, he was making it clear that Hanna was here with him.

'She's a good friend, Katarina,' he said, giving the tour guide one of those crinkly-eyed looks, along with that charming smile of his. 'We found, quite by chance, that we were attending the same conference and I bought another ticket for her because… well…' Mac lowered his voice and Hanna knew the effect it was probably having on a woman who was younger than she was. 'You know how it is when you don't want to say goodbye to someone too soon?'

Katarina might have fallen under Mac's spell, but it was only long enough to accept Hanna's presence with a resigned nod.

'Please get on the bus immediately,' she instructed, as she made a note on her clipboard. 'We depart in exactly three minutes. The driver will attend to your luggage.'

Katarina stood at the front of the bus, holding a microphone, as it pulled away exactly three minutes later.

'Our first stop will be at Amberg,' she told the group. 'We will visit the Sanctuary of Maria Hilf, which is a notable cathedral. You will be able to enjoy this attraction at your leisure for forty-five minutes. For the benefit of today's newcomers, I ring a bell when it's time to get back on the bus. Please do *not* be late as it will disrupt our itinerary for the rest of the day.'

Hanna bit her lip, her gaze flicking up to meet Mac's. She didn't have to say a thing and a quirk of his eyebrow told her that he knew perfectly well that her inner rebel had just been triggered. The look also suggested that she should go with the flow and might even find she was enjoying herself.

Like the way he'd looked at her as he'd trapped her hands late last night, when they'd finally escaped the dinner to get back to his room. She'd been putting her arms around his neck so that she could kiss him sense- less but he'd caught her wrists and held them above her head as he took firm control of this private greeting. Hanna had stepped back to find herself against the wall, her hands still above her head as Mac proceeded to kiss *her* senseless and it had been the start of an- other, astonishing physical encounter. Hanna could feel herself melting inside just thinking about it and she knew that her gaze was softening. Giving in. Agreeing that 'going with the flow' might be a good thing in this new adventure.

'A delicious morning tea will be provided in a nearby restaurant,' Katarina continued. 'After that, we will travel to Lauf an der Pegnitz for a tour of the picturesque capital of the Nürnberger district, in Bavaria. Lunch will be provided there, and I will tell you about the afternoon's activities at that point. Please sit back and enjoy the ride. I have many interesting things to tell you about along the way.'

Mac had insisted that Hanna take the window seat so there were many interesting things for her to see along the way. She didn't turn her head again, but she moved her hand to where Mac's was resting on his thigh. She slid her hand beneath his and curled her fingers over his. She could feel both his initial surprise and then, a softening on his part as well. Perhaps he was giving in to the experience of having company.

Someone to share an adventure with. This might be only going to be a brief, holiday relationship but Hanna wanted it to be something special for both of them. And she was going to make sure that Mac never felt lonely.

Nobody had ever, ever held Hamish Mac-Millan's hand.

Not when he was a child and certainly not as an adult.

He almost pulled it free but something stopped him, and within a very short period of time he was very glad he hadn't. To outward appearances, Mac was looking through the window and enjoying the same scenery that Hanna was. In actual fact, he was barely aware of the countryside they were travelling through because the warmth of that human touch that had nothing to do with anything sexual was stealing through his entire body, stirring up an emotional response that was initially so difficult to define that he gave up trying and decided to simply enjoy another new experience.

It wasn't until Hanna withdrew that apparently casual link between them, as they climbed off the bus at their first stop, that he realised how deep that response had actually been.

Because he could feel the absence of it even more than its presence?

Because it made him feel lost? Abandoned, even? Was it possible he had memories he'd never known he had, from being rejected as an infant and given away to be raised by people with whom he had no biological link? When he'd been separated from the sister he'd been able to touch since he was aware of being alive? Perhaps he'd held hands with his twin sister when they'd been in their mother's womb, like he'd seen photographs of unborn twin siblings doing.

And, perhaps, that was what made holding hands with Hanna feel like he'd found his way home…

Mac shook off the notion as being no more than an overreaction to a different physical experience as he followed the group to gather in front of the church. Katarina was holding up a large, artificial sunflower.

'You will be able to see this—my favourite flower—at all times,' she said, looking directly at Mac and Hanna. 'The rest of the group had practice yesterday, but this is new for you both. Please stay close, so you will be able to hear all the information I have to share.'

Hanna tilted her head to speak in a whisper to Mac even though the group was already climbing the stone steps to the entrance. 'What about the forty-five point seven minutes for us to enjoy this notable attraction at our own leisure?' She looked as though she was trying not to laugh aloud. 'Before the bell rings to make us get back on the bus.'

'Or possibly salivate?' Mac whispered back.

That did make Hanna laugh. The sound made Katarina turn and even from this distance they could see that they were the subject of a disapproving look. Churches were clearly not the place to be laughing aloud but the reprimand made Mac feel defensive on Hanna's behalf. Why would anyone want to stifle the sheer *joie de vivre* with which Hanna approached life—the kind of positive energy that made her such a delightful companion?

He found himself hanging back, reluctant to follow the group inside and contribute to stifling anything and it seemed that the universe agreed as a raised voice nearby caught both Mac's and Hanna's attention.

'Lucy…stop that right now. Do *not* push your brother.' A mother had two small children who were fighting over something.

The girl was obviously not taking any notice of the instruction and, moments later, the younger boy was taking a tumble down the long flight of stone steps. He landed with a bump and, after a beat of shocked silence, let out a piercing shriek.

Hanna was already halfway down the steps, reaching the child at the same time as his mother. Lucy was now crying as well.

'Oh, my God… Thomas…are you all right?'

Mac joined them. 'Making this much noise is usually a good sign,' he told her.

Hanna was watching as Thomas threw himself into his mother's arms. 'His movement's not restricted in any way. And I couldn't see any bumps on his head.'

Both children were still wailing. Hanna held out her hand to Lucy. 'It's okay, sweetheart,' she said. 'I know it was an accident. Do you need a cuddle, too?'

She did. Hanna sat on the step beside the mother with Lucy in her arms. Thomas calmed down enough for Mac to give him a quick check.

'Can you wiggle all your fingers for me? Like this? Does anything else hurt?'

Thomas wiggled his fingers and shook his head.

'Let me see if I can feel any bumps on your head.'

Hanna could actually feel how gentle his touch was as he examined Thomas for any sign of a head injury. Not that she needed any confirmation of the kind of skills he had as a doctor, but it was heart-warming to see how good he was with small children.

Thomas wasn't crying any longer but he was clinging to his mother like a small monkey. 'I think I need an ice cream, Mummy.' There was still enough of a wobble in his voice to persuade his mother.

'Thank you so much for your help,' she said, as she prepared to leave with both her children. 'I knew that sightseeing in a church probably wasn't the best idea with these two. We'll go ice cream hunting instead.'

Mac sat down beside Hanna on the step. 'Would you prefer an ice cream, too?'

Her smile made him an accomplice in her reprieve from the tour group. He liked that. Rather a lot, in fact.

'Can we go for a walk instead? Over there?'

'You're good with kids,' Mac said, as they

walked towards a patch of forest on the far side of the car park.

'So are you.'

'But you really like them, don't you? If you were Thomas and Lucy's mother, you'd probably be giving them a holiday adventure in this forest, not dragging them into an ancient church.'

Hanna laughed. 'Yep. That would be much more fun for me, too.'

The patch of forest was cool and green and deserted. After the busy flow of tourists and the noise of crying children, the peace and quiet of being amongst the trees was more than welcome. It also had the invitation of a private, almost intimate, space. It was peaceful. Safe. Mac remembered the moment when he'd begun to feel this safe in Hanna's company—when she'd told him that she wasn't interested in marriage or kids. There was a note of sadness in the thought that she'd never be that amazing mother providing adventures for small people, though.

'Have you never wanted any kids of your own?'

'Can't have them.' Hanna's tone was dismissive. 'I had an emergency hysterectomy when I was sixteen so that I didn't bleed to death.'

'Good grief...what happened?' Mac was taken aback by what must have been a traumatic, life-changing injury. It also seemed somehow disappointing that such a vibrant, warm person was never intending to create a family of her own.

'It was an ectopic pregnancy,' Hanna said quietly. 'My gran might have been right to think that only ballet or ballroom dancing was okay. I got pregnant to someone I met in a salsa class.'

'That's a terrible thing to have happened... I'm so sorry.'

'Don't be.' Hanna offered him a smile. 'It happened a very long time ago and, on the plus side, I spent so long in hospital I discovered that I really, really wanted to become a nurse. I also discovered that I didn't actually want to have kids at all. The whole idea of parenthood was so scary it was a relief to know I'd never have to go there. It felt like a "get out of jail free" card.'

'Of course it was scary. You were no more than a kid yourself.'

'But I haven't changed my mind since then. Even when it turned out to be a deal-breaker for the guy I thought I was going to spend the rest of my life with and I tried to change my mind, I couldn't. We talked about surrogacy and adoption and all the different ways it's possible to create families these days.'

'You can't change how you feel about something that big because someone else wants you to.' Mac blew out a breath. 'And if you have to change that much to try and make a relationship work, it's doomed anyway. It might not have felt like it but it would have been far less painful to find that out, make a clean break and move on.'

'Wow...' Hanna's glance was curious. 'Sounds like you're speaking from experience.'

'You could say that.' Mac drew in a long, slow breath. 'Coincidentally, it was an accidental pregnancy that made me realise I didn't want kids, either.'

Hanna blinked at him. 'No way... How old were *you*?'

'Nineteen. In my first year of med school.' Like telling Hanna about his unknown sister, this was something else Mac had never shared with anyone but this was a connection that was on a very different level. How many people could understand how confronting it was to be faced with parenthood when you were barely out of childhood yourself?

'There was no choice about accepting it,' he told her. 'Not for me. Not when it was my first serious relationship. I was in love. I thought we could make it work but my girlfriend had other ideas. She wasn't going to give up her career or her life for a baby she wasn't ready to have. She only told me she'd gone and had an abortion on the day she broke off our engagement. That was when I made my real choice.'

'That you didn't want to have kids?'

'That I was the only person who was going to make any decisions that might change my own life. And the only way to be sure of that is to do it by yourself.'

Any relationship was dangerous. Because if you loved someone and you wanted to be loved, you were handing control of a significant part of your life over to them. If they didn't feel the same way, they could destroy too much.

Hanna was nodding slowly. Of course she got it. She wasn't chasing any dream of marriage and kids. She was living her life exactly how she wanted to, wasn't she? Independently. Adventurously.

And maybe it was the opposite side of the coin to the way he'd chosen to keep his life meticulously organised and predictable but, on a fundamental level, it felt like they were kindred spirits. How lucky were they to have this unexpected time to enjoy being with the company of someone who could understand and accept them for who they were?

'This works, though, doesn't it?' Mac said softly. 'I think I approve of holiday flings.'

Sunlight was filtering through the canopy of the trees in visible, misty rays that caught Hanna's eyes. It lit up the sunburst of colour around her pupils, before her iris became a mix of gold and brown and green that collided with that dark rim.

Extraordinary eyes.

Eyes that were as unique as Hanna Peterson.

He remembered her looking up at him like this last night, when they'd finally reached his room. When he'd caught her wrists and held her captive, like some sort of caveman, pushing her up against the wall and giving in to the desire to kiss her until a lack of oxygen forced him to stop long enough to take a breath, only to start again and, this time, to hold her wrists with one hand so that he could use his other hand to find her most intimate point of pleasure…

What was it about this woman that made him totally unaware of the kind of inhibitions he'd always had when it came to sex because giving in to desire like this was its own form of losing control? Good grief… he was thinking of doing it again, right now. Backing her up against the trunk of a tree in broad daylight when they could be discovered by anyone at any moment.

Just a kiss would be okay, though. Wouldn't it?

Hanna seemed to think so. And it wasn't until they could hear the blaring of a loud horn that they finally remembered where they were.

'Is that the bus?'

'I think so.' Mac could see the way Hanna was trying to blink off the drugging effect of their kissing. 'We'd better run. I didn't hear the bell, did you?'

'No. Oh, dear… Katarina is not going to be happy.'

Katarina was, in fact, furious. 'It is entirely unacceptable to disrupt the timetable of everyone else on a tour they have paid for,' she told them. 'And I will not allow the reputation of my company to be tarnished. If this happens again, the bus will not be waiting for you.'

Katarina wasn't the only person who was less than happy. Mac and Hanna had to get past the highly annoyed glares of everybody already well settled in their seats as they made their way to the back of the bus.

It should have been highly embarrassing.

It really shouldn't have made Mac feel as if he was finally tapping into a teenaged rebellion he'd completely missed out on experiencing.

Would it have been this much fun back then?

As he slid into his seat and caught Hanna's gaze, he decided that the answer to that was a resounding 'yes'—it would have been, if she'd been his partner in crime.

A little while later, when they were on their way to the next stop on their tour and Hanna's hand once again crept over to take hold of his, Mac squeezed back without hesitation.

Yes…this felt like coming home. To something familiar and beloved.

And then it hit him.

Was he breaking what had become an ironclad barrier and falling in love with someone again? Was it because Hanna didn't seem to have emotional barriers of her own that it hadn't occurred to him to ensure that his own were firmly in place?

And, if he *was* in danger of falling in love with Hanna Peterson or it had happened already, was it really something to be worried about when he was enjoying himself *this* much? It was only for a few days, after all.

A mere blink in his lifetime.

'I'm really sorry, Mac.'

They had both known the bus would have long since left without them but staring at Mac's suitcase and Hanna's backpack, abandoned by a stone wall in a corner of the parking area and under the amused gaze of other tourist bus drivers, made it all too clear that Mac's holiday was in ruins.

'This is my fault,' Hanna added. She bit her lip as she sat down on the top of the wall. 'We should have stayed with the rest of the group and Katarina and gone shopping in the marketplace.'

'To buy souvenir lederhosen or cuckoo

clocks?' Mac's snort was dismissive. 'I doubt that we would have been welcome at the restaurant they were all having lunch at, either. We weren't the most popular people on board, were we? We were the disruptive latecomers.'

Was it her imagination or was there a note of pride in Mac's voice? Hanna couldn't imagine that being punished for unacceptable behaviour was something that he was familiar with. That glimpse into his childhood of being so captivated by the meticulous workings of a clock suggested that he had been a very intelligent and probably extremely tidy and well-behaved youngster. Was he looking at this as part of his new experience of travelling with company?

An adventure?

Thank goodness he didn't seem to be furious with her. Or was he skilled at hiding how he really felt?

'Will you be able to get your money back?'

'I doubt it.' Mac shrugged. 'It doesn't matter.'

'It is my fault,' she said. 'It was me who suggested that a balloon ride would be fun.'

'And my choice to make it happen.' Mac met her gaze and...yes...there was definitely a hint of amusement making his eyes sparkle. 'We're equally at fault, here.'

That was true. Hanna would never have spent so much money on a short ride in a hot air balloon to see the sights of this city, like the castle and other historic buildings lining the riverbanks, from above. She should have protested more but, to be honest, she'd loved that look in Mac's eyes that told her he wanted to pay for it—that it would be a pleasure to give her something she would enjoy. It also looked as though it was meant to happen, because there was a balloon that seemed to be getting ready to take off and… well, why not see if they had the space to take another couple of passengers?

By skipping the group lunch, they would still be back in plenty of time to catch their bus, so they bought their tickets and climbed into the basket, clutching each other's hands as flames roared and ropes were dropped and they rose slowly into the air. It was certainly the best way they could have seen the sights and, really, it was no one's fault that wind conditions unexpectedly changed and blew them off course so that they ended up in a farmer's field some distance away and had to wait for the balloon company's van to come and collect them.

'What do you think we should do?' Hanna asked.

Mac laughed. 'I was hoping you'd tell me,' he said. 'I've never been expelled from a bus tour before. Didn't you tell me how much you liked to arrive somewhere and follow your nose?'

'Mmm…' Hanna took out her phone and opened a browser. 'Nuremberg airport is only about fifteen kilometres from here,' she told him. 'That seems like a good place to start. I can call a taxi to get us there.'

'Where do you want to fly to?'

Hanna caught his gaze. 'Where would *you* like to fly to?'

'I'm something of a beginner in nose-following.' Mac was showing nothing on his face, but his gaze was holding hers with that intensity Hanna was starting to love. 'Surprise me.'

Did that mean Mac was not only happy to let her take the lead but that he was still happy to spend the next few days in her company? She needed to make her choice a good one, then. Hopefully, an experience Mac would remember for the rest of his life and one that would erase any of her own guilt about her part in ruining his bus tour. She clicked to open another window and began scrolling.

'There are direct flights from Nuremberg to quite a few destinations,' she told him. 'It'll be up to chance what seats are available but today, it looks like we could potentially end up in Cyprus, Athens, Istanbul or Barcelona.'

'And we just go? Without even a hotel booking?'

'Nose-following.' Hanna nodded, her tone serious. 'I've never ended up sleeping on the streets,' she added. 'But there's always a risk that adventures might not turn out to be quite what you expect. Are you up to taking that chance? Living a little dangerously for a few days?'

He was holding her gaze again, so intently it felt as if he was searching her soul, as he was deciding whether to take that risk. It was obvious that behaving so impulsively was totally out of character for Mac but she knew that already about him. And she knew why he'd learned that he needed to have as much control as he possibly could over his life. He might not have been ready to be a husband or father when he was only a teenager but it must have been an absolute betrayal to have the future he'd chosen to accept torn away from him. She could understand why he had never trusted another woman that much again but…but she wanted him to trust her. Just for a little while, at least. For the few days they had planned to have together before they both returned to their real lives and never saw each other again.

Hanna couldn't make any promises about how things might turn out by taking him on an unplanned adventure but she could hold her own breath and hope that he would choose to come with her. Choose to trust her…

Maybe that hope was showing in her eyes because Mac's gaze softened as his lips curved.

'What is it about you?' he murmured. 'That makes it impossible to say "no"?'

CHAPTER SIX

THIS WAS A new planet for Mac.

A world away from a well-run emergency department or even the kind of rules that kept his personal life organised and efficient. This was a world where responsibilities could be abdicated, and rules ignored. You could eat whatever you liked without considering its nutritional value, take a few days away from reality and not feel guilty about ignoring almost every email and dismissing increasing tension from any approaching commitments and deadlines. You could even give someone else the control of where you might go and what you might do when you got to the mystery destination.

The destination chosen at Nuremberg airport had ended up being Barcelona and they'd arrived so late that evening there was only time to find a hotel, but it became clear the next morning that there were going to be small adventures they were going to find each day and more rules that could be broken.

Okay…there did seem to be one rule that was unbreakable and that was that time—like life—was short and it had to be made the most of. A large part of that process appeared to involve living in the moment and Mac was learning that he'd never quite known how to do that before meeting Hanna Peterson.

Perhaps it had been something he'd learned *not* to do when he was too young to understand what a protective mechanism was and how to use it. And then it became something to juggle in his work life when he had to be aware of every single thing happening in each moment of a medical emergency but he also needed see a bigger picture of what could have happened to lead up to this situation and how to manipulate what was going to happen next in order to provide an acceptable outcome.

He'd never learned to simply *be* in the moment and savour it. To feel things on an emotional level and find joy that made that moment something to treasure. Like the taste of his chocolate and mint ice cream that he'd almost finished by the time Hanna finally found the perfect patch of sand to sit on and dropped the sandals she'd been carrying in her hand.

'How good is this?' She beamed. 'I had no idea that train was going to bring us to the beach.'

'We might have ended up in France,' Mac agreed. He'd been carrying his shoes, with the socks stuffed into their toes, to follow her example of walking barefoot on the sand and, along with that taste of chocolate and mint, he'd been aware of the movement of soft sand trickling between his toes.

He watched Hanna chase a drip of ice cream and capture it with her tongue and felt a different kind of lick happen in his gut. Good grief…it was a revelation that desire could actually increase when you kept having sex with the same person. Or was that because the person was Hanna? Because he was visiting Planet Hanna where so much of life was about the senses and emotions. Bohemian stuff that he'd stayed well clear of in his life so far.

She was nodding in response to his comment. 'That's actually not a bad idea,' she said. 'We could go there next. Have you ever been to Corsica? Isn't that where the French Foreign Legion hangs out? There might be a ferry we could catch.' Her glance was mischievous. 'If I'd lived in those days, I might have disguised myself as a boy and joined the Legion to go and have adventures.'

'That doesn't surprise me in the least,' Mac said. 'I imagine you get bored with real life.'

'Not at all.' Hanna brushed a stray curl of her hair out of the way of her ice cream. 'I love my job. I wouldn't want to work anywhere other than in the emergency department, though—where you can never know what might be coming through the door next. Don't you love that adrenaline rush?'

'I've almost forgotten what it's like,' Mac admitted. 'And I'm missing it. I've spent too much time being no more than a guest in someone else's ED while working on my latest thesis.'

'What was the subject of your research?'

'In a word, bruises.'

He could see the moment and the impressive speed with which Hanna joined the dots.

'Paediatric injuries? Non-accidental?'

Mac gave a single nod. 'I'm working on guidelines for an updated screening tool that will hopefully mean that it's easier to identify at-risk children. There's a lot of technical stuff comparing methods of imaging as well. Conventional and cross-polarised, infrared and ultraviolet.'

'Ultraviolet like they use in crime scenes to show up blood or other body fluids?'

'It can also be used to identify trauma that may have happened months ago. And infrared imaging can give us additional information about injuries below the surface of the skin. It can cancel out the effect of a higher level of melanin in the epidermal layer, too, which makes it particular useful on bruises that can be invisible on darker skin.'

'I did a postgraduate course on triage in the ED a while back,' Hanna told him. 'Part of that was a set of tools to help us differentiate between accidental and intentional bruising. The TEN 4 guidelines?'

Mac nodded. 'Bruises on the trunk, ears or neck on a child under four years old.'

'And any bruise at all on a baby under four months old.'

'If they can't cruise, they can't bruise.'

It was Hanna who broke the rather subdued silence that fell between them.

'That speech you gave to open the conference—I was so close to tears with your story.' She seemed unaware that melted ice cream was starting to drip onto her fingers. 'I've seen that little boy myself, more than once, and…it's heartbreaking.'

Yes… Mac could see that heartbreak in her eyes and that, in itself, was a revelation about this woman. She could live in the moment even when it was distressing, and she could embrace that emotion as much as she captured and celebrated something positive like joy. Life was a roller-coaster for Hanna but she wasn't about to miss any of the ride.

'I'm still haunted by the first case I saw,' Hanna continued. 'I'd just started in the ED and the mother of this toddler was so upset because she'd only taken her eyes off him for a minute, she said, and he'd managed to climb onto the table and then fallen off. He'd hit his head and had a seizure. I was trying to comfort her. I was telling her it wasn't her fault.'

Mac let his breath out slowly. He knew what was coming.

'One of the doctors noticed there was something odd about the shape of his elbow. And one of his legs was swollen. When they did a scan they found half a dozen fractures.

Social Services got called and then the police. The mother blamed her boyfriend but it turned out to be both of them. I couldn't believe it. I couldn't understand how anyone could deliberately hurt any child, let alone a baby. I've never forgotten it. I always have it at the back of my head with every paediatric patient I get.'

'Me, too,' Mac said quietly. 'When that kind of trust in people is broken, it never comes back, does it?' He cleared his throat. 'But that's a good thing. It means that you're more likely to pick up cases of non-accidental injuries and get a child out of an abusive situation.'

'Mmm…' Hanna still sounded subdued. 'Was he a real case that you were involved with, that little boy in your story?'

'Yeah…' Mac closed his eyes for a heartbeat. He couldn't tell her how real, though. He knew better as an adult, of course, but there was a level of shame that never quite vanished. That feeling that it was somehow his fault that it happened.

That he'd never been good enough. Or really wanted. That the people who were supposed to love him couldn't be trusted.

'I hope he got all the help he needed,' Hanna said.

'I believe so. Eventually.'

'I bet he grows up to become a doctor,' Hanna said. 'Because he felt like someone cared about him in the ED?'

Mac shrugged.

'I wish I could have looked after him,' Hanna said softly. 'I wish I could have given him a cuddle and made him believe, even for a little while, that he was special.'

Oh...*man*...

With the kind of control that Hamish MacMillan had over his life—and his emotions—it would be unthinkable to cry in private, let alone in a public place or in front of someone, but he had a lump in his throat that felt like a bit of broken glass. He remembered the initial shock of Hanna holding his hand on that bus ride—of a physical touch that had nothing to do with sex. Of feeling that he wasn't alone. That someone cared about him. It had been disturbingly powerful as an adult. To have felt anything like that as a small, frightened child must have been completely life-changing.

Hanna had finally noticed the remains of her melted ice cream and dug a hole in the sand to bury it. Then she got to her feet, a thick layer of sand covering her hands.

'I need to go and find a wave to wash my hands in. I might even have a paddle if it's not too cold. Coming?'

Of course he was. Moving would be the best way to clear that jagged lump he could still feel in his throat. Besides, Hanna had just wound another thread around his heart and it felt like he needed to stay close so they didn't break just yet. She might have no idea of the chord she'd struck by her compassion for that little boy in his story but Mac had the odd sensation that he was being truly seen for the first time for who he truly was. That this bond he'd found with Hanna was more real than anything in his life before this.

A reality that was, ironically, completely separated from his real life. Mac knew his time in Hanna's world was short but that was a bonus in itself, because it gave him the freedom to make the most of every moment.

Hanna had reached the wash of waves on the sand and just walked in, not caring that the hems of her jeans were getting soaked. She swished her hands in the water and looked up to smile at Mac.

'It's not cold at all,' she told him. 'Not in

comparison to the liquid ice we get in Dunedin even in the middle of summer. Do you reckon we could get away with swimming in our undies?'

And, just like that, the moment changed from one that had echoes of the sadness associated with such a grim topic of conversation, and a somewhat disturbingly intense feeling of connection to another person, to one of pleasure in the feeling of sunshine warming your skin and the fizz of seawater rushing over your feet. To the grounding and a reset of mood that being in the moment could provide.

Mac dropped his shoes and strode towards Hanna and he was laughing as he scooped her up into his arms. She wound her arms around his neck and they were lost in their kiss as the next wave and then another rolled in around his feet.

The past evaporated and the future was invisible and whether or not this was what being in love was all about didn't matter. Mac just wanted to bottle this moment and keep it for ever so that, when he needed to in future, he could take the cork out and live in this moment again, even if it was just for a heartbeat.

Because *this*...

This was what most people considered to be the holy grail of being alive, wasn't it?

Finding out what happiness felt like.

Mac had always been of the opinion that the pursuit of personal happiness was not only futile because it was usually so fleeting, it was also supremely selfish.

Now, he was beginning to wonder if he'd got it all wrong...

Barcelona was a magic city.

Or, perhaps, the magic came from a combination of the company Hanna was lucky enough to have, the gorgeous summer weather and the unexpected delights that surprised them around every corner.

They lost count of how many times they walked up and down La Rambla and explored the fascinating alleyways that led off from Barcelona's famous tree-lined central street. They wandered hand in hand through the bustling marketplace with its astonishing array of meat, vegetables, cheese and flowers and sampled every different, delicious variety of tapas they could find in the cafés and restaurants. They were excited by a wonderful Salvador Dali exhibition they came across quite by accident and they marvelled at still unfinished Sagrada Familia, the iconic work of Spain's most celebrated architect, Gaudi. What Hanna loved most of all, however, was another of Gaudi's creations—the Park Güell. From the fairy tale, gingerbread houses with their white icing roofs at the entrance, past the stunning mosaics and up the hill into the soft, green spaces of grass and trees, it was a wonderland.

The surprise of finding a busker, sitting beneath a tree at the side of a gravelled path, playing one of her favourite songs on a twelve-stringed guitar as he sang, was a moment of pure joy for Hanna. She stopped and stared for a moment and then dropped her shoulder bag, unable to resist the urge to dance. The ruffled layers of her summer dress swirled around her legs as she twirled, her arms in the air, but it was the look on Mac's face as she saw him watching her that took this space and time to a completely different level.

If she'd stopped to think, Hanna might have remembered that Mac had told her how much he'd hated dancing lessons at his boarding school but she was acting on impulse when she caught his hands and perhaps the surprise was enough to suck him into this bonus moment of magic. Whatever the reason, she knew instantly that he had either paid attention to those lessons or he was a natural dancer. And that he'd forgotten that he'd believed dancing could never be enjoyable.

He held her in his arms and they danced in the dappled shade, lost in the music and the lyrics. Hanna's arms were bare and the touch of Mac's hands skimming her skin as he sent her away from his body and then twirled her and gathered her close again added to her total immersion in this unforgettable moment. Maybe they weren't dancing in the dark, or barefoot on the grass like the lyrics they could hear, but it still felt as if they were an integral part of this romantic song—as if it had been written for them—and Hanna found herself closing her eyes as their dancing slowed until they were merely swaying together.

Was it Mac who dipped his head to touch her lips with his own, or did Hanna go up on tiptoes as she lifted her face to his?

Whatever...

It was just fortunate that Hanna still had

her eyes closed. That Mac wouldn't be able to see any reflection in her eyes of what was in her mind right then. In her heart. In every damned cell of her body, in fact.

She knew this feeling and had been prepared for it to surface. She'd known at the end of her first day with this stranger who was practically her polar opposite that she was probably halfway to falling in love with him and she'd also known that her heart had been even more firmly captured by every new thing she learned about Mac. Experience had taught her that holiday flings could accelerate emotional involvement or create a depth that would never have been there if they'd met in real life but, even knowing all of that, Hanna had not expected anything like this. She'd never felt it take hold of her quite like this, with a power that was almost frightening, and Hanna knew why.

Because she and Mac had a connection that could change everything. Hanna couldn't have children. Mac didn't want any. For the first time since Hanna had had her heart well and truly broken long ago, it seemed as if it might be safe to fall in love. To dream of a future?

Except that she knew that the kind of future she was thinking of was the last thing that Mac wanted in his life. He was travelling alone. By choice. And she could understand why when the first time he'd been shaping a new future as a husband and father, it had been shattered by someone he'd loved. It was no wonder he felt the need to be in control—to keep himself so buttoned up. A few days of a perfect holiday was hardly likely to change his mind about the way he lived his entire life. Was it…?

Maybe Mac felt the ripples of what Hanna was feeling even if he couldn't see her eyes. Perhaps even the musician was aware of what was hanging in the air surrounding them because the music suddenly faltered and the spell was broken. Or it could be that Hanna's imagination was running away with her and she was the only person with an emotional overload. She was the only one who'd tripped up and fallen in love.

Mac found money to drop into the busker's open guitar case, Hanna collected her bag from where she'd dropped it and they simply carried on with their walk as if nothing momentous had just happened.

But something *had* happened.

Something had changed.

In the same way Hanna had sensed that the attraction between herself and Mac was the kind best suited to a holiday fling because it was going to erupt into fierce flames, she could feel the moment that it began to burn itself out.

On Mac's part, anyway.

'What will you do next?' he asked as they walked on, the music behind them fading. 'You've still got two weeks before you fly home, yes?'

'I do.'

Two weeks of travelling.

Alone. With the freedom to go anywhere she chose and experience whatever new adventures each day could present. But, for the first time ever, there was no excitement to be found in the prospect and that was more disturbing than the realisation of how hard she had fallen for Hamish MacMillan. Hanna needed to ground herself again, urgently, before she lost any of the pleasure that anticipating this trip had given her. She took a deep breath and found her brightest smile.

'I shouldn't admit this because it's not really in the spirit of nose-following, but I think I do have a bit of a plan.'

'Which is?'

'I liked my idea of catching a ferry to Corsica. There should be another ferry that goes to the south of France on the other side of the island and then I could drift down into Italy. Or I could jump from Corsica to Sardinia and skip France.' She threw Mac a glance but kept her tone casual. 'Want to see if we could find a ferry later? You could have at least a day in Corsica.'

The tiny hesitation on Mac's part made Hanna's heart sink. 'I think it might be a flight I need to find. I've been reminded that there's a satellite symposium happening in Amsterdam the day before my next conference. I had an email from a colleague who's hoping to meet me there.' Mac's steps were slowing. 'I didn't say anything because...' He stopped and faced Hanna. 'I wanted more time with you. But it can't last for ever, can it? Isn't that the definition of a holiday fling?'

Hanna managed to smile even though she could feel her heart already beginning to break.

'I'll never forget this,' Mac said softly. 'I'll never forget *you*, Hanna Peterson.'

'You'd better not.' Hanna made her tone stern as she started walking again. 'You've learned how to follow your nose now.'

Her inward breath caught somewhere in her chest. She wasn't about to forget any of this, either—including how buttoned up Mac had been when she'd met him in front of that clock. She'd never have imagined him walking into waves on a beach and getting his tidy trousers stained with seawater or dancing in a public park and kissing her so passionately in broad daylight. There was something sad in the thought that he might go back to his real life and this time together would be no more than a memory for him.

'You need to let yourself be impulsive more often, Mac. Take a risk or two.' She caught his gaze over her shoulder because this was important and she needed to know that he was listening. 'Remember that clock that you love so much and use it to remind you to find the time to do something new. Or to do something that you've thought of doing but you've never got around to it.' She offered him another smile. 'You'll never know what you might be missing out on otherwise.'

Mac watched Hanna walking a little ahead of him, heading downhill, which would lead them to the way out of this astonishing park.

He wanted to catch her hand and pull her to a stop again but he couldn't. What if it made him feel like he had moments ago when she was dancing with him to that guitar music? When it felt like another moment of the kind of happiness he'd experienced on the day they ate ice creams on the beach? What if he ended up risking too much by saying what he was really thinking?

Mac might tell her that these few days had changed everything. That he felt like he might be falling in love with her and he couldn't bear the thought of never seeing her again. But…she hadn't disagreed with him when he'd said that it couldn't last for ever. That this was no more than a fling. She already had plans for the rest of her holiday and it wouldn't surprise Mac at all if she met someone else along the way. Someone who was more like herself and could embrace the kind of freedom and openness and ability to live life to the absolute limit that was such a part of Hanna's soul.

He wasn't about to spoil anything for her by making their parting difficult in any way and he wasn't about to make a fool of himself by suggesting that this was anything more than Hanna believed it was so it was just as well he was a master at hiding his feelings. He'd been telling the truth when he'd said he'd never forget her but he had his doubts about following her advice to take more risks in his life. Risk was the opposite of control, after all, and he'd spent his life keeping as much control as he could to avoid exactly that.

Control kept you safe from the kind of emotions that, right now, were threatening to become unpleasantly overwhelming so the sooner he got on with restoring familiar levels of normality the better. Mac pulled his phone from his pocket, opening a browser as he continued walking.

Because it wouldn't hurt to check if there were any flights from Barcelona to Amsterdam later today. If nothing else, it would be a good first step in the right direction. Back to the ordered reality of his own planet, which might lack the same levels of personal indulgence and pleasure but at least it was safe.

And being safe was almost the same thing as being happy.

Wasn't it…?

CHAPTER SEVEN

'HANNA… THANK GOODNESS you're back. I've missed having you around.'

'I've missed being around.' Hanna hugged Jo back—as best she could over a now impressively pregnant belly—and found herself very unexpectedly blinking back tears, which, of course, her best friend noticed instantly.

'You okay? Did something happen on your holiday?'

Oh…where would she start? Yes. Something had indeed happened on her holiday. Something huge. An emotional roller-coaster like no other and the plunging dip that had started when she'd said goodbye to Mac was apparently still going despite her homecoming yesterday. The ride had been bumped up at times on her continued travels but, despite Hanna's determination to make the most of a trip she'd been looking forward to so much, those temporary lifts had only seemed to speed up the next dip into a very unfamiliar, *lonely* space. At some point in the near future, she might have to stock up on wine and chocolate and have an evening with Jo to tell her everything.

Outside the internal double doors that led to Dunedin's Princess Margaret Hospital's emergency department, when they were about to start a morning shift was certainly not the time to even hint at such personal woes.

'It's just jetlag.' Hanna smiled as she hung her stethoscope around her neck. 'And, on top of that, I got home to find my flatmates had a big party last weekend. They hadn't noticed that someone had crashed in my bedroom so I had to change my sheets and do a full load of laundry before I could even start unpacking.'

'Ew...' Jo made a disgusted face. 'I don't know how you can still cope with flatting.'

'I'm beginning to wonder myself.'

'My wee house has got a temporary tenant, but it'll be available to rent again sometime soon if that's an option. I might even sell it before the end of the year.'

Hanna loved Jo's quirky cottage but...

living alone? When she was currently trying to get used to a loneliness like nothing she'd ever experienced before? She needed to change the subject.

'Are you and Cade still loving your new house on the peninsula?'

'Oh, yeah...you'll have to come and see it. Maybe we can have a last barbecue before winter sets in properly. I need to show you our holiday photos, too. I'm still on a high from that idyllic beach. It was perfect...'

'I'm so glad.' Hanna was looking through the glass panels of the doors. 'Looks busy in there. I'd better get to work.' She pushed one of the doors open and gestured for Jo to go ahead of her but Jo shook her head.

'I've got to duck up to Admin. There's some final paperwork for my maternity leave to sign off. Officially starts today, actually—I'm just here to tie off some loose ends.'

'Any luck with the locum?'

'Mmm...' Jo was already turning away but there was an odd gleam in her eyes as she threw a glance over her shoulder. 'I wanted to let you know who it was before you got back but Cade thought it might be a nice surprise. They're rostered on today for second shift so you'll find out soon enough.'

'It's someone I know?'

But Jo was already on her way to where she needed to be and only raised a hand in farewell. Hanna stepped through the doors into ED and immediately forgot about it. As the charge nurse for the upcoming shift, she needed a detailed handover so that she was on form to supervise the department's nursing staff and use any opportunity to teach the less experienced nurses. She would also have to field any patient complaints, liaise with specialists for consultations, keep an eye on medical supplies and be available at all times for a trauma code. On the plus side, not only would she have no time to think about her own emotional state, her jetlag would be well and truly dealt with by the time Hanna had coped with the next nine hours. She could then go home and crash and, with a bit of luck, life would seem far more back to normal by tomorrow.

Shifts were arranged to overlap so there wasn't a complete changeover that could disrupt the continuity of patient care so Hanna had been working for a couple of hours before the second shift started. The department was busy enough for her to feel she was totally back in the swing of things so she was unprepared for the blow that came completely out of the blue. Feeling pleased that she'd found time to give one of the new nurses a tutorial in placing leads to take a twelve lead ECG on a cardiac admission, she felt it like a body blow to glance across the department and see the back of someone reading the electronic census board, which was the access point for any operational and patient-related information.

Someone tall, with dark hair, who was standing with commendably good posture, which made them look an awful lot like Hamish MacMillan.

Hanna had every reason to go and check the board herself and make sure that the requested consult with the cardiology department was now recorded for the patient she'd just seen but she found her steps slowing as she approached. Because this was more than simply seeing someone that reminded her of Mac. The weird tingling sensation that was getting stronger with every passing second was surreal. The realisation that Mac was, in actual fact, standing right in front of her—

giving her that crinkly-eyed intense look and *smiling* at her—was overwhelming.

'Hey, Hanna…'

She couldn't say anything. For that first, long moment of suspended time, all Hanna was aware of was a joy like no other. A feeling that the huge, empty space she'd been living with for the past two weeks had suddenly vanished. Filled by the physical presence of the man she felt so strongly about. Her words came out in no more than a whisper.

'Mac…what on earth are *you* doing here?'

As she spoke, Hanna could feel the wash of something that felt like…anger?

How on earth was she supposed to get over how she felt about Mac if she had to go back to square one again?

'I followed my nose,' Mac said. His voice was low enough for nobody else to hear. 'And I put my hand up to be Jo's locum.' He hadn't broken their eye contact. 'At least for a while. You did tell me I should do something new.'

'Yes…but…' Hanna was lost for words. He hadn't needed to come to the other side of the world to do something new. Had he come this far because *she* was here? With another twist, a flash of hope cut through her tumbling emotions. Perhaps Mac had been following his heart and not his nose?

'Hanna?'

The tone of the person calling her from the central desk made Hanna turn her head swiftly. She could feel that kaleidoscope of her own feelings evaporating instantly.

'Ambulance notification.' A senior nurse was putting down the dedicated phone. 'Penetrating mechanism chest injury. Systolic BP less than ninety. Heart rate greater than one twenty. Shall I initiate a trauma Code Red?'

Hanna was there in no more than a few steps. 'Yes. What's the ETA?'

'Four minutes.'

There wasn't much time and it was Hanna's job to get everything organised. Alerts had to go out to members of the team. In addition to the most senior emergency consultant available in the department, they needed an anaesthetist, radiologist, a surgical consult on standby and all the usual staff for a resuscitation area. The blood bank needed to be contacted and have blood products and thawed plasma available. Hanna wanted to ensure that a rapid infuser was primed and ready for use in Resus and that an ultrasound machine was at the bedside. A check that tranexamic acid—to reduce or stop traumatic haemorrhage—was amongst the available drugs was also high on her list.

'Who's on as trauma team leader today?'

'Jo. No, wait…it's her locum.' The nurse must have noticed something in Hanna's expression. 'Don't worry. Word is that he's the best.'

It was Mac's first trauma call on his first day of this locum position in a small—by international standards—hospital at the bottom of the globe. With his level of expertise and experience, it shouldn't be anything out of the ordinary but Mac was aware of a heightened alertness that made this somehow more significant.

Because this was the first time he would be, officially at least, working with Hanna Peterson and…he wanted this to be successful. Impressive, even? Or to erase what had looked disturbingly like a flash of something like fear in her eyes when she was struggling with unexpectedly seeing him again?

Whatever. There was no time to spare even another thought about Hanna as Mac donned his PPE and tried to familiarise himself with this new resuscitation space as rapidly as possible.

Finding that the paramedic bringing this critical trauma case into the department was one of the only three people Mac had ever met from this city helped ground him. And Cade's handover was giving him vital information about this case.

'This is Sean Watson. Forty-one years old. Forestry worker who got caught by the canopy of a falling tree. A branch penetrated the left side of his chest, third intercostal space, leaving a puncture wound but no visible impaled object. BP is currently one hundred over sixty-five, up from eighty-five over sixty on arrival. Suspected tension pneumothorax but fluid seen on ultrasound did not suggest a cardiac tamponade. He's had bilateral decompression but he's having increasing difficulty breathing. GCS thirteen on arrival but probably twelve now.'

'Oxygen saturation?'

'Variable. Between eighty-six and ninety-four.'

'Sean...can you hear me?'

The patient groaned beneath his oxygen mask. He opened his eyes but his agitation made his speech hard to understand. His skin was grey and he was clearly terrified.

'You're in hospital now,' Mac told him. 'We've got you, okay?' He glanced at the team around him, including Hanna, who seemed to still be assigning roles. A scribe was ready to record everything, a nurse was stationed beside the drugs trolley and an orderly was standing by, probably to deliver bloods samples to the laboratory and bring back the products that might be needed from the blood bank.

'Let's get him onto the bed,' Mac directed. 'I'd like to do another ultrasound.'

His FAST examination—the Focused Assessment with Sonography in Trauma—confirmed Cade's impression that there was no blood to be seen in the area around the heart, which was consistent with other signs like the patient's neck veins not being distended. That they were dealing with a life-or-death situation became more apparent in the short time it took to use the bedside ultrasound, however. It was Hanna who called out the warning that Sean's blood pressure was falling rapidly and it was only seconds later that their patient lost consciousness.

It was Hanna who assisted the airway doctor when Mac made the call to sedate and intubate Sean and he could see her in his peripheral vision, efficiently checking and then administering the drugs needed and then providing the assistance like pressure on the cricoid cartilage to aid the passing of the endotracheal tube. At the same time, she was clearly supervising the setup of the O negative red blood cells and the thawed plasma and Mac was relieved to have them available when he made an incision in the chest wall to try and get to the blood that was accumulating internally.

Even in a space full of people who were accustomed to dealing with major trauma, there was a collective gasp as an estimated blood loss of more than two litres happened the moment Mac opened the anterolateral incision he'd made. The resus area immediately took on the appearance of a war zone but the glance he caught from Hanna as she positioned herself beside him to assist was calm and the silent message perfectly clear.

I'm here. What do you need?

'No pulse,' the airway doctor warned.

With the direct vision Mac had of the heart, he could see that it had stopped beating. He placed one hand behind the heart and the other in front and began a rapid squeezing motion from the apex upwards. The movement was easy to continue automatically, as Mac controlled the chaos around him. Blood products were being rapidly infused, the patient was being ventilated. Drugs were being drawn up and blood samples sent for analysis including rapid measurements of oxygen levels. Vital signs measurements were called out for the scribe to record. Pauses in the cardiac massage initially revealed the potentially fatal rhythm of ventricular tachycardia but, at one point, after drugs were administered, it reverted to a normal sinus rhythm, which gave everybody the hope that this dramatic emergency department intervention might be one of the few that could succeed.

Except that Sean was still losing blood. Eight units of blood and fluids had now been infused but the blood loss was ongoing and it was impossible to see where it was coming from.

'I can see it pooling on the front wall of the ventricle.' Mac pressed the swab Hanna passed him against the outer wall of the heart to try again. 'But I can't see the puncture wound.' He caught Hanna's gaze. 'I'm going to have to open the sternum.'

A single nod and Hanna opened a new sterile roll onto the trolley to hand Mac a scalpel, then a bone saw and then retractors. This was a desperate last attempt to save this patient's life and Mac wasn't about to think about how unlikely it was to be successful. Especially when he could now see the two-centimetre hole in the right ventricular wall.

'Suture, please, Hanna,' Mac said quietly. 'And we'll need a Teflon patch if we've got one. I want to get this as secure as possible before we shift to Theatre.'

Against all odds, that was what they managed to achieve only a short time later, as Sean's blood pressure finally started to rise to an acceptable level as the injury was closed and his heart was able to start beating normally to restore his circulation.

Mac went with his patient to Theatre but, as the senior consultant on duty in the department, he couldn't stay to watch the surgery. He did have to take the time to completely change his scrubs, though. Even the best PPE hadn't been enough to prevent the bloodstains. The resus area would be out of action for a while as well—there was a team still cleaning up as Mac arrived back in the ED.

Hanna was the first person he saw as he walked through the doors and, this time, there was none of the shock he'd seen on her face earlier this morning. He could see the hope in her eyes first of all and he nodded.

'It was still looking good when we got him into Theatre. Sinus rhythm, systolic BP just over a hundred.'

The consultant who'd been in charge of Sean's airway and ventilation came past and stopped to offer Mac a handshake.

'First time I've seen that happen successfully,' he told Mac. 'That's some way to introduce yourself, mate.'

'Yes. Welcome to Dunedin, Mac.' Hanna was smiling. 'We're lucky to have you here.'

He could see admiration in her gaze, but Mac shrugged off the praise. 'I'll be waiting to see what the post-surgery ultrasound can tell us about heart function. And whether there are any neurological sequelae. Where am I needed next, Nurse Peterson?'

And there it was…

A flash of something extremely personal and a very long way from being unpleasantly surprised to have him appear in her life again. An acknowledgement of the astonishing physical connection they'd discovered with each other in Europe, if nothing else, which was one of the reasons he'd talked himself into finally visiting this far corner of the globe.

Because he'd started missing Hanna Peterson the moment his plane had taken off from Barcelona.

She was the one to break the eye contact. 'Let's have a look at the board,' she suggested. 'I'm not going to tempt fate by mentioning the "Q" word but it might be possible for you to grab a coffee. Do you know your way to the staffroom?'

'I do. Perhaps you might be due for a break as well?'

The glance he received was speculative. 'Perhaps. I have to say I'm looking forward to finding out what persuaded you to come and be Jo's locum.'

'It was you,' Mac told her, as they stopped in front of the digital board.

The glance he got this time was startled. Disconcertingly, he could see something in her eyes that reminded him of her silent query for an update on their dramatic chest-cracking case—a question that was steeped in hope... Had he said too much? The wrong thing? Was she taking it to mean something too personal, which would be unwelcome given that she had spelled out her feelings about marriage and, presumably, any committed relationships? He tried a wry smile to defuse any tension.

'You told me to do things I'd thought of doing but never got around to, remember?' Mac kept his tone offhand. 'Well, visiting New Zealand was definitely one of those things and when I remembered Cade mentioning the locum position to cover Jo's maternity leave, it seemed like fate, as well as you, were giving me a bit of a nudge.'

'Ah…okay…' Hanna's smile looked a little forced. 'I guess I can't take all the credit for being responsible for you being here to save a life in such dramatic fashion on your first shift, then.' Her gaze shifted as she looked over her shoulder. 'I'd better go and check on the clean up in Resus One and order any new surgical supplies to restock. You should go and have a coffee while you can.'

In the flash of time between Hanna turning towards the resuscitation area and when she actually began to move, Mac's thoughts tumbled one on top of another at the speed of light.

He knew he'd definitely said the wrong

thing that time. He could feel the protective barrier that Hanna had suddenly activated around herself.

He'd been trying not to alarm Hanna with the idea that he'd come all this way because the pull to see her again had been so powerful but it had been a stupid thing to say, anyway, because Mac didn't believe in fate. It was coincidence, rather than fate that he'd met Hanna and her friends and discovered that there was a locum position in a country he'd thought of visiting long ago. A position that just happened to fit with an unexpected gap in his professional life.

Like risk, the idea that fate could determine what happened in your life was in the category of being the opposite of being in control and he'd left Barcelona with every intention of re-establishing exactly that kind of control.

It had been a conscious, controlled decision to come to New Zealand.

Or had it?

If Mac was really honest with himself, his decision had been very much influenced by things he was struggling to control—namely the way being with Hanna had made him feel. How much he had missed being with her and how badly he wanted to see her again. It was more than simply 'wanting', however. Mac could feel a *need* to be that close to the only person he'd ever met who made him feel connected to another human on such a significant level. Someone who could see him for who he truly was. Maybe a part of what had driven his impulsive decision was wondering whether the way Hanna made him feel was simply a part of a fantasy that came from being on holiday with the total freedom of seeking nothing but pleasure in their surroundings and each other's company.

If it was something that evaporated in real life it would make it so much easier to move on and not be haunted by…what…the feeling of having thrown away something truly significant? More important than anything else in his life so far?

He had stepped into Hanna's real life and, so far, that feeling hadn't changed at all. If anything, working with her had made it feel even more as if they were kindred spirits. Two halves of the same whole?

'Hey…' His soft call made Hanna pause. Just for a heartbeat but it was long enough. 'There was another reason, as well.'

She didn't say anything but she lifted her gaze to meet his with a question filling her eyes.

Mac kept his voice low enough that it was no more than a whisper. Only Hanna could hear him.

'I couldn't stop thinking about you,' he said.

CHAPTER EIGHT

MAC *HAD* COME all the way across the world because she was here, hadn't he?

He might have convinced himself that it was a combination of other things that had led to him deciding to come to this small country at the bottom of the world, but Hanna wasn't fooled. Okay, maybe he did have an unexpected gap in his professional life that was providing a kind of sabbatical leave and time to do things he might not have otherwise considered. There was also his newfound appreciation of following his nose instead of planning everything he did in his life, including travel, to the nth degree, and, of course, an unexplored curiosity about where his twin sister had been raised. And maybe he'd needed to fool himself in order to feel safe making his choice, but it had been a simple combination of words that had made Hanna's heart sing.

I couldn't stop thinking about you...

The way she hadn't been able to stop thinking about him? Snatches of memories that had coloured so many moments of every day since she had last seen him? And every single night?

Memories of conversations. Of laughter. Of emotions that could steal her breath without any warning. Feelings that could make everything look so much brighter, like the joy of being in Mac's arms when he'd whirled her around in the waves of that Spanish beach or the tenderness as he'd held her so close when they'd danced under that tree in the park. The sheer enormity of the love that filled her heart with every memory was both a blessing and a curse.

Hanna had spent the rest of her holiday in Europe trying to find a way to stop those feelings morphing into the pain of heartbreak.

And now, she had to find a way to stop reading too much into what she'd seen in Mac's eyes when he'd told her he hadn't been able to stop thinking about her. Or into what was happening so unexpectedly by his arrival in her normal life. She needed to be careful not to say too much, too. Even when, late that evening, she found herself holding her breath as she waited for Mac to open the front door of the little terraced Victorian house that Jo had made available for him to rent.

Hanna knew it well. She loved the high ceilings with their decorative plaster work, the beautiful, tiled fireplaces with solid, wooden surrounds, the polished floorboards and the narrow staircase that led to the cosy bedrooms upstairs. Not that she was thinking of any of the features of this small house as the door closed behind her. Hanna wasn't even aware of where she was, in fact.

This could have been a hotel room in Prague for all it mattered the moment that Mac's gaze captured hers and the rest of the world was shut out. It could have been a private patch of forest in Germany or a beach in Barcelona. Place was irrelevant because there was something else that Hanna knew so well it felt like it was imprinted on her soul.

This...*desire*. The magnetic pull that was so strong it felt like surrendering to it was the only way to ever feel whole. All she needed to do was to stand on tiptoes so she could brush his lips with her own. Except that she didn't need to stand on tiptoes, did she? Because Mac was waiting for it and then, suddenly, he wasn't waiting. He was the one who was moving. Dipping his head and covering her mouth with a kiss that tasted like…

Oh…what *did* it taste like, exactly? She had all the time in the world to decide, as one kiss melted into another with no more than a heartbeat of a gap between them that provided the gasp of a new breath or a blazingly intense beat of eye contact. The knot of sensation deep in her gut grew until it was too big to be in one place. It unfurled and spread until it seemed to touch every cell in her body and then it threatened to scramble the ones in her brain, but not before she realised that she knew the answer to the question she'd asked herself.

These kisses tasted—and felt—like Hamish MacMillan.

It was that simple.

And that complicated.

Because it wasn't just that she'd seen—and *felt*—that connection in his eyes when he'd told her he hadn't been able to stop thinking about her. She'd seen the shadows as well and it had broken her heart. She'd sensed the fear of being vulnerable and giving someone else the opportunity to hurt him.

To reject him, even?

Maybe it went even further back than his broken first love. Maybe it was something a lot deeper. Had he always lived with a feeling of having been rejected because his mother hadn't kept him?

To have come here at all was a huge step for Mac to have taken and she knew it had a tentative shape to it. Good grief, he'd been enough out of his comfort zone to take the risk of their impulsive travel to Barcelona. A wrong word from her carried the risk of planting or nurturing any seeds of doubt he might well already have and the last thing Hanna wanted was for Mac to do a U-turn and vanish from her life again.

Falling into his arms again like this might be a risk but Hanna could no more prevent herself from taking it than from taking her next breath. That Mac already trusted her enough to have crossed the world to see her only made Hanna love him even more. She was not about to do anything to break that trust.

She knew that Mac needed to hang on to all those other reasons he'd used to persuade himself to come this close again. He wasn't ready to think any further ahead than the weeks, or months, of this locum position he'd chosen to take. And she was happy to give him that time. And yes, there was hope to be found—of course there was—and a glow of happiness that had already obliterated the downside of jetlag and any trace of heartbreak.

This extra time together felt like a gift for them both. An appropriate one, even, considering they'd met in front of one of the world's most famous clocks. And, like she'd said, when they'd had the time to explore Prague together, she didn't want to waste a minute of it.

Mac had learned long ago to avoid impulsive decisions of any kind and that included how he might feel about any given situation. It wasn't that he didn't have the ability to make split second decisions and then act on them because that was a part of his job and he was confident that those rapid decisions could be justified because his experience meant he could gather facts and figures and predict what the outcome might be.

That confidence was purely associated

with professional decisions, however. Personal ones, especially to do with anything emotional, were a very different story but Mac had perfected a method of making those decisions as well. He kept a safe distance behind well-constructed barriers until he could control any emotional reaction and then he could make well-considered choices that were both practical and unlikely to cause problems in the future. It had always worked particularly well when it came to his relationships with women and there were a few ironclad rules.

He'd never had a liaison of any kind with someone he worked with on a regular basis. Spending time in their company was always a well-planned, often formal, occasion such as a show or dinner. And a sexual encounter was never in his own bed because, that way, he was always in control of when he chose to leave.

He'd given himself permission to ignore all those rules when it came to Hanna Peterson because it was only going to be a temporary lapse of good judgement, but it could be argued that that could also apply to being here in New Zealand. Like a holiday fling, a locum position had a definite endpoint that was clearly on the table and that meant that working with Hanna was an exception to that rule.

Sharing his own bed with her was another exception because it appeared to be the only option for whatever private time together they were able to find.

'You don't want to come to my place,' Hanna had told him. 'Apart from it being horrendously untidy a lot of the time, one of my flatmates—Amanda—is a Theatre nurse here and you know what hospital grapevines can be like with a bit of new gossip.'

Mac liked the fact that Hanna didn't want people talking about them. A lot. It not only made it feel like they had something special that was purely their own, but it felt as if Hanna respected his need to be in control of his own life.

His first couple of weeks in Dunedin were so busy they passed in a flash. He needed to get up to speed with different protocols for patient treatments, how the department was run and to get to know his new colleagues. Out of work hours were also busy as Mac learned his way around a new city and dealt with life admin like sorting a vehicle and shopping for essentials. Having been invited to cover Jo's position as a HEMS doctor if needed, he had training sessions with the local emergency helicopter service to sign him off on their operational requirements.

It became apparent that Hanna wasn't even talking to her closest friend Jo about what was going on because Cade clearly had no idea that Mac had anything more than a professional relationship with Hanna. Cade was looking apologetic, in fact, as he pushed an empty stretcher past where Mac was signing a patient's discharge summary that Hanna was waiting for.

'I'm so sorry we haven't had you out to dinner yet,' Cade told Mac. 'I've been working too many shifts and Jo's pretty tired what with getting the house set up for the baby. I hate to think you might not feel as welcome as you are.'

'It's not a problem,' Mac assured him. 'I'm still settling in.' He smiled at Hanna as he handed back the paperwork. 'And I'm being very well looked after.'

'That's good to hear.' Cade also smiled at Hanna. 'Jo said to invite you to dinner as well. It's been ages and we haven't even seen your holiday photos yet. Did I hear you went to Barcelona? And Corsica?'

'Mmm...' Hanna was already turning away. 'Tell Jo I'll call her soon. We've got lots to catch up on.'

Cade began moving away, too, but then turned back. 'I was telling our station manager about that disaster response triage workshop you ran in Prague and he got excited by the idea of running one here. Any chance you'd be up for sharing your expertise?'

'Count me in,' Mac said. 'There might be ED staff that would be interested as well. And what about the fire service here or the police? It can be very useful to combine a training exercise that involves extrication and possibly police exercises. I've still got a template for a scenario based on a terror attack that we used in Scotland. It brought all the emergency services together, with the police clearing the area first, then the fire service managing extrication from collapsed buildings and ambulance coming in to do the triage at the end. A fair bit of work to set up but I remember we got great feedback from that one.'

'Sounds perfect.' Cade reached for his pager that was beeping loudly. 'I'll organise a barbecue in the next few days and we'll talk more.' He glanced at the message on his pager. 'Gotta run,' he said. 'MVA on the motorway. Car versus motorbike.'

It wasn't just a new hospital in a new country that Mac was experiencing. With the boundaries of his rules blurring he was in a strange space that straddled professional and personal elements. It had aspects of the unfamiliar, like a holiday, but it was most definitely the real, everyday life he'd been working in ever since he graduated and there was nothing quite like having to deal with all the good, the bad and the ugly that an emergency department could provide in the way of caseloads and challenges.

Working, sometimes very closely, with someone he knew intimately and was coming to trust on many levels was also a completely new space to be in and...

And it was a revelation.

Working with someone whose brain worked as quickly as his own and was on the same wavelength enough to sense and communicate urgency without saying a word. When that person could anticipate what he needed and provide the kind of support required without instructions, obstacles that could slow down his interpretation of the overall picture and what needed to happen next were removed. It almost felt like he had an extra pair of hands that were as trustworthy as his own and, when an emergency began unfolding, that could tip the balance firmly in favour of saving a life.

Like it did only a day or two later when Mac sensed Hanna's concern about a patient she was with when he happened to be walking past the cubicle she was in with a young, female patient. When he caught her glance, it reminded him of when they had met for the very first time—when they had exchanged that glance that was a mutual acknowledgement that something significant was happening to their tour guide, William, and it was about to get more serious.

On first glance, Hanna's patient did not seem to be particularly unwell.

'This is Alisha,' Hanna told him. 'She's twenty-nine and her friend brought her in to Emergency because she was getting some chest pain and she's a bit short of breath. Alisha, this is Dr MacMillan.'

Mac unhooked his stethoscope from around his neck. 'Can I have a quick listen to your chest?' he asked.

'Sure.'

'Lean forward a little for me?'

'Heart rate's one ten and regular,' Hanna told him as he positioned the disc of his stethoscope on Alisha's back. 'Respiration rate is twenty-four, SPO2 is ninety-four per cent on room air and her blood pressure is one-oh-five on seventy. I was about to do a twelve-lead ECG.'

Mac nodded. 'Good idea.' Age was no guarantee that chest pain might not be cardiac.

He lifted his stethoscope as Alisha coughed and then coughed again. When he saw the tissue she pressed to her mouth, Mac could feel the hairs on the back on his neck prickle slightly. A rapid upward glance revealed that Hanna hadn't missed the bright smear of blood on the tissue.

'Have you had any trauma recently?' Mac asked. 'Like a broken leg or a bad bruise?'

'No.'

'Any surgery?'

'No.'

'Long haul flights?'

Alisha shook her head. 'I should be so lucky,' she said. 'I haven't had a holiday in a long time.'

'Any chance that you could be pregnant?'

She shook her head. 'I'm on the pill.'

Hanna knew exactly what Mac was thinking—that Alisha might have a pulmonary embolus and/or a deep vein thrombosis. She had ripped open a plastic bag and was plugging the end of the attached tubing to the plug on the wall that was an outlet for the main oxygen supply.

'I'm going to give you a bit of oxygen,' she explained to Alisha. 'It should help your breathing. We might get you out of your jeans, as well. Have you got any pain in your legs?'

Alisha nodded. 'My left leg was sore when I got up this morning.'

Her leg was swollen and red as well as tender.

'It's possible that you've got a blood clot that's formed in one of the veins in your leg,' Mac told her. 'If bits of it are breaking off, it would explain what's happening in your lungs.'

'A clot?' Alisha's eyes widened in fear. 'That's really bad, isn't it?'

'You're in exactly the right place to get it sorted,' Mac said. 'I'm going to do an ultrasound on your leg, which will tell us if something's happening. We'll do an X-ray of your chest, too.' He turned to Hanna. 'We'll need an arterial blood gas measurement soon but I'd like to get an IV in first.'

It didn't surprise him that Hanna already had the IV trolley in the cubicle. With deft movements, she opened drawers and gathered everything he would need. A tourniquet, alcohol wipes, a cannula and sticky patch to cover it, a syringe and an ampoule of saline to flush the line. She was moving rapidly enough for Mac to see that she was sharing his sense of urgency, even though her manner was completely calm.

'This is nothing to worry about,' she told Alisha. 'We're going to need some blood samples to help us figure out what's going on with you and if we have a line in, it means we don't have to poke you again if we need to give you some medication.'

Alisha was coughing again as Mac slid the cannula into place. Hanna began taking another set of vital signs as she finally flopped back against her pillows.

'I feel kind of dizzy,' she told them.

'Systolic blood pressure's dropped,' Hanna informed Mac. 'It's less than ninety.'

Alisha had her eyes closed now. They could see from the movements of her chest wall that her respiration rate had increased noticeably since the coughing.

Mac stepped towards the end of the bed and lowered his voice. 'We've got a PERT available, haven't we? A Pulmonary Embolus Response Team?'

'Yes. It's a collaboration between specialities that's activated from here. It's your call.'

Mac gave a single nod. 'Let's do it. I'm comfortable that a Wells score puts the priority for a PE as high. I'm going to get an ultrasound of her leg and set up a heparin infusion but I'd like the team here asap.'

Bleeding risk needed to be assessed and a decision made about using clot-busting thrombolytics to treat the clot, if it was indeed as big as Mac suspected, or whether surgery or catheter-based techniques would be used before Alisha was admitted to the Intensive Care Unit.

In the end, the young woman was administered catheter-directed drugs to treat the massive clot and then mechanical removal to clear her vein. If any residual areas were narrow enough to potentially cause a recurrence, she might need further treatment with angioplasty and stenting.

'They've placed a filter in the inferior vena cava to prevent any further PEs.'

Hanna seemed fascinated by the images Mac was able to show her that evening when they were discussing the case. And this was another huge bonus of a relationship that went beyond being colleagues. Mac loved a good debrief.

'It's only temporary. Once things are stable, she should be able to take blood thinners.'

'How did you know that the clot was so massive? I can't believe it went all the way from her calf to her groin.'

'I didn't. And I probably should have taken the time to properly rule out all the differential diagnoses, too.'

'Such as?'

'Aortic dissection. Tension pneumothorax. Triple A.' Mac was counting them off on his fingers. 'Ectopic pregnancy.'

'You sounded like you knew.'

'I was trusting my instinct. Also, I've never forgotten a case I was involved with treating when I was a med student. The guy was being thrombolysed and I was monitoring him when he had a syncopal episode that started just like when Alisha began feeling dizzy.'

'What happened?'

'His heart rate and breathing rates went up and he was going blue with hypoxia. A minute or two later and he was unresponsive and pulseless. You can imagine how panicked I was.'

'Did he survive?'

Mac shook his head. 'Which is why I've always remembered him. Huge PE on both sides and a massive clot that disabled the right side of his heart. Did you know that seventy per cent of patients who have a fatal PE die within the first hour of the onset of symptoms?'

'I do now.' Hanna blew out a breath. 'And I won't forget it, either.' She smiled at Mac. 'There you go...for the rest of my working life, whenever I see someone who might have a DVT, I'll be thinking of you.'

Oh... Mac liked that idea. The whole benefit of any debrief was that lessons were learned and perhaps a different case in the future would benefit.

He liked the way Hanna was looking at him right now, too. It was obvious she'd had enough of talking about work and it was time for the kind of wind down from a busy day that could take them both to a place that had nothing to do with anyone but each other. The expression on her face reminded him of...what was it? Oh, yeah...that time when they were in front of the clock in Prague and he'd told her that she looked like a dog who couldn't wait to be allowed off leash.

He also told her, in a somewhat round-about fashion, that he thought she was beautiful. And he realised that being here, in this space between holiday fantasy and real life, wasn't, in any way, changing what he thought about this astonishing woman. She was just as enchanting. Just as captivating as the first moment he'd noticed her outside that hotel in Prague.

'Do you know,' he said softly. 'I suspect I'll be thinking of you for the rest of my life whenever I see a clock.'

'That's way more romantic than a DVT.' The smile curving the corners of Hanna's mouth was reaching her eyes and making them distinctly misty. 'Okay... I'll think of you whenever I hear someone talking about Barcelona.' Her gaze dropped to his lips. She was thinking about kissing him, wasn't she?

'Or see people dancing, perhaps,' she added softly.

'It was the best holiday,' Mac said. 'The best fling.' He was looking at *her* mouth, now, savouring the moment before that imminent kiss. 'We should do that nose-following thing again.'

'Mmm… When?'

'Next summer?'

'Northern hemisphere summer or southern hemisphere summer?'

Mac lifted his gaze. 'Why not both?'

Hanna laughed as she leaned closer. 'I like the way you're thinking.'

Her lips brushed his, a soft butterfly kiss that was teasing him into making the first move and Mac needed no more encouragement. In the heartbeat before he began what was becoming a familiar but no less delicious prelude to their love making, he was realising something else.

That Hanna was the perfect woman for him. They shared a passion for the same career in emergency medicine and would always, always have interesting things to discuss. They both loved travel. The sex, that had been the best ever from that first night, wasn't losing any of its attraction and, perhaps the biggest connection of all, they both felt the same way about marriages and families of their own.

Like the locum position Mac was currently in being a blurred area between real life and a holiday, the idea of going away with Hanna twice a year was like a soft-edged space between a relationship and a holiday fling.

It could be safe.

Perfect, even…?

CHAPTER NINE

'Is THERE SOMETHING going on that I should know about?'

Hanna tried a surprised expression on Jo but she should have known that her best friend would see straight through it.

'Oh, my goodness…there *is* something going on, isn't there?' Jo's smile was growing. 'You can thank me later for helping choose him for covering my maternity leave.'

Hanna cast a glance over her shoulder from where she and Jo were sitting on a couch in front of the bay window with the amazing view out to Dunedin's picturesque harbour, but Mac was still busy in the kitchen of Jo and Cade's house, opening the bottle of wine they'd stopped to buy on their way here.

'To be honest,' she said, 'it started in Prague.'

'*No*… You didn't say anything.'

Hanna bit her lip. 'Maybe I didn't want to

admit I'd jumped into bed with someone the first day I'd met them.'

Jo laughed. 'Hey…no judgement here. It was the first date for me and Cade. There's no getting away from that kind of chemistry.' Her glance in Mac's direction was thoughtful. 'It's that good, huh?'

'Gets better every day,' Hanna murmured.

Not just in gradual increments, either. After that evening last week, when Mac had suggested they had two summer holidays together every year, there was a new, stronger thread that was binding their connection even more tightly.

Because it suggested permanence.

Not in the normal sense of a couple choosing to spend the rest of their lives together but Mac was never going to ask Hanna to marry him, was he? Or suggest that they lived together. So this…the idea that they would meet up, to have a wonderful adventure somewhere, was probably the closest he was ever going to come to committing himself to a significant relationship.

And it was enough for Hanna.

Enough to fill her heart with the kind of joy that could only come from being in love. From knowing, deep down, that Mac was feeling the same way. Even if he wasn't admitting it, even to himself. She could feel it in the way he touched her when they made love and now, because he was thinking of ways they could be together in the future.

Perhaps Mac could sense that he was under observation. He looked up from where he was pouring red wine into two glasses.

'What can I find for you, Jo?'

'There's some orange juice in the fridge. I'd like that diluted with some soda water, please. Half in half.'

'No worries.'

Jo grinned at Hanna. 'He's starting to sound like a Kiwi.' She lifted an eyebrow. 'He might decide to stay?'

Hanna shook her head. 'I don't think so.'

But the idea of Mac leaving as soon as his locum finished wasn't scaring her. After all, it was only a short time ago that she thought all she would ever have with Mac were the memories they had already made. His idea of all those holidays to come was giving her a whole future of opportunities to keep making memories and, when they weren't together, they could be staying in touch and planning for the next time and that would be enough to keep this joy alive.

Wouldn't it?

Jo was distracted by the vibration of her phone on the coffee table. 'I hope that's Cade,' she exclaimed. 'He should have been home half an hour ago. He's the one who's supposed to be doing the barbecue.'

She read the message and groaned.

'What's up?' Hanna asked.

'He's been stuck. The patient he was called out to see was deceased by the time he got there and he had to wait for the police to arrive. He's only just heading back to the station.'

'Oh, no...' Mac had heard Jo as he came in with the drinks. 'That sounds like it could take a while?'

'We won't wait for him. I'm sure you'll be able to drive the barbecue, Mac.' Jo put her glass down on the table. 'I can get it going to warm it up.' She started to get up from the sofa but fell back with an even louder groan than reading the message had elicited.

Mac frowned. 'Are you okay?'

Jo nodded, but her eyes were closed. 'It's getting harder every time,' she said. 'I've had trouble staying on my feet today because it makes my back ache and then, when I sit down, it's too hard to get up.'

'Don't move,' Mac instructed. 'I'll sort the barbecue.'

'And I can do the food,' Hanna said.

'There's not much to do.' Jo still hadn't opened her eyes. 'There are some salads in the fridge, fresh bread that just needs slicing and a potato bake that's already in the oven. The sausages will take longest so they need to go on the grill first. There's steak and bacon as well.'

'Sounds delicious,' Hanna said. 'But let's wait a bit before we start cooking in case Cade gets away soon. Or are you starving?'

'I'm not even hungry,' Jo confessed. 'I don't think there's any room in my belly for food now.' Her smile was wry. 'Remind me why I thought it was a good idea to get pregnant at my advanced age?'

'Advanced age?' Mac raised his eyebrows. 'What... I thought mid-thirties was the usual age these days.'

'Mid-thirties?' Jo laughed as she threw Hanna a meaningful glance. 'I can see why you fell for this guy.'

There was a beat of something in the air that Hanna had not expected. It felt like Mac was startled—as if it hadn't occurred to him that Hanna might have fallen in love with him? She didn't dare meet his gaze but, from the corner of her eye, she could see that he hadn't moved a muscle. He was still focused on Jo.

Jo shook her head at Mac. 'I'm forty-six,' she told him. 'So this is my one and only shot at motherhood. You're not likely to see a primigravida more elderly than me.'

Mac blinked and that odd frisson that Hanna had been aware of evaporated.

'Okay... I'm impressed,' he said. 'Even more so that you travelled all the way to Europe when you were *how* many months pregnant?'

'Close enough to six. But I wouldn't have gone if there'd been any complications. The trip home was the hardest. I got such a backache on the plane that Cade was scared I was going into labour.'

'When's your due date?' Mac asked.

'Not soon enough,' Jo sighed. 'I've probably got at least another four weeks of this.' She used the arm of the couch to haul herself properly upright as her phone began to ring, leaning forward to grab it from the coffee table.

'Cade?' She listened for a moment. 'Okay... No speeding.' She was smiling as she ended the call. 'He's on his way,' she told her guests. 'And he loves a run on the peninsula road on that bike of his. He won't be...'

Jo's smile was being overridden by a grimace that suggested severe pain. Mac did look up to catch Hanna's gaze this time, but he wasn't thinking about anything Jo had said. This was the kind of glance that was becoming familiar. The one that signalled a level of alertness when an internal alarm had sounded. The sort they'd exchanged within minutes of meeting before their tour guide had collapsed. Just like the more recent occasion when Mac had realised that their patient with the pulmonary embolus might be critically unwell.

But this was about Hanna's best friend and there was no reason to think that she was in trouble, was there?

'Do you need something for that back pain?' she asked. 'Have you got a heat pack or a hottie somewhere?'

'I'm fine.' Jo was getting to her feet. 'I just really need to go to the loo. An empty bladder will help.'

She had a hand pressed to her back as she tried to straighten up but she didn't lift her head and Hanna was aware of another strange beat—as if the universe was holding its breath. The feeling intensified as Jo spoke slowly.

'Uh-oh…'

She was still looking down and Hanna shifted her gaze to see what Jo must have felt happening. There was fluid soaking her leggings.

'Did I just wet myself or is it what I think it might be?' Jo was sounding perfectly calm as she lowered herself back onto the couch. 'Han…would you mind getting a towel or two out of the linen cupboard? It's in the hall, beside the bathroom.'

Hanna could hear Mac sounding just as calm as Jo as she rushed out of the room.

'Tell me about this back pain of yours, Jo. When did it start? Give it a score out of ten…'

The soft, clean towels Hanna grabbed were a pale, oatmeal colour. In the time it took to put them between Jo and the couch, the faint bloodstains were obvious.

'I think we should call an ambulance,' Mac said.

'No…' Jo shook her head. 'Cade will be home any minute. It's quite normal for there to be a bit of blood in amniotic fluid and it's also normal for contractions to not even start for twenty-four hours after waters break. There's no need to panic.'

Except that in the silence that followed her words, there was an odd expression appearing on Jo's face.

'I can feel something weird,' she said quietly.

Hanna felt her heart sink. 'What sort of weird?'

'Pulsatile weird,' Jo whispered.

'Okay...' Mac was rolling up the sleeves of his shirt. 'Let's get you lying down, Jo, and find out what's going on.'

It was Hanna who helped remove Jo's lower clothing so she was the first to see the loop of umbilical cord. They all knew the implications of a cord prolapse. The oxygen supply to the baby was in danger of being cut off by pressure from the baby's head and it could be catastrophic. Severe oxygen deprivation could lead to brain damage or death. They all knew the recommended management, which was to keep the pressure off the cord until the mother could be rushed into Theatre for an emergency Caesarean section. And they all knew that being this far away from hospital was a significant addition to the risk factors. It was Hanna who helped Jo turn onto her knees, putting her head down to let gravity help with easing the pressure on the cord. As she moved away to call for an ambulance without alarming Jo, she was grateful to hear the reassurance in Mac's voice.

'I'd say you're very close to being fully dilated. I can feel baby's head.' He still sounded calm as Hanna returned within a few moments. 'Okay…you're going to feel me pushing a bit now that the head's far enough down to elevate. It's a good thing you've got a full bladder. That's going to help take pressure off as well.' He looked up at Hanna. 'What's the ETA for the ambulance?'

'Ten to twelve minutes,' she said quietly.

Jo groaned. 'I knew there had to be a downside to living in a place where you got a panoramic view of the city in the distance.'

'It's okay,' Mac said. 'Guidelines for the diagnosis to delivery time for a cord prolapse is less than thirty minutes. The team will be waiting and we can get you straight into Theatre.'

Cade had clearly got through any traffic with ease, thanks to his motorbike. He came through the door of his home only minutes later and his training and experience as a critical care paramedic gave him the ability to take in both exactly what was happening in his living room and the potential implications. Jo was his absolute priority, however. He knelt beside her on the floor to support her physically and, more importantly, emotionally.

'We've got this,' he told his wife. '*You've* got this…'

'Oh, God…' Jo cried out a minute later. 'I need to push…'

'Hang on.' Mac's voice was too calm now. His features were set in lines that Hanna hadn't seen before. Grim lines. This wasn't part of any recommended protocol. Even if Jo was fully dilated, an assisted delivery with forceps was needed to make it as fast as possible. In order to deliver the baby, the measures being used to protect the blood and oxygen supply through the umbilical cord, with the position Jo was in and the pressure Mac was keeping on the baby's head, would have to be abandoned and, as soon as that happened, the countdown would be on.

The potential need for a neonatal resuscitation was another factor they needed to consider because the only resources they had available were the combined skills of the people here. People who would have to cope without the benefit of the kind of specialist medical equipment that might well be needed to save a tiny life. People who were all too aware of the stakes involved.

None were more aware than the parents of this longed-for baby that was trying to arrive in a very less than desirable way.

Jo cried out again and this time, there was a note of agony in the sound. 'I *really* need to push...'

'We've got two options,' Mac said. 'We try and slow the delivery until we can get to hospital or we try and speed it up.'

Hanna watched as Cade and Jo locked gazes on each other. She knew how huge this decision was. How precious this baby was to both of them. Having been so closely involved in the wedding and even the honeymoon of her best friend, Hanna had learned a lot about a love story that was so powerful it was easy to believe it was meant to be. She knew that this pregnancy was quite likely to be Jo's only chance to become a mother and that Cade had already had the devastating loss of an almost full-term baby, long ago. There was such intensity in the way they seemed to be communicating silently.

There was also so much love it was palpable enough to bring the sting of tears to the back of Hanna's eyes.

And the decision was made. It was going to take too long to wait for the ambulance, try and keep stalling delivery for the return trip to the hospital and then to get to Theatre. Whether delivering the baby here, as fast as possible, carried less risk was a terrifying choice to make but it was one the parents made together.

With the first signs of the next contraction, Jo was turned onto her back, half sitting, cradled in Cade's arms as he knelt behind her. Hanna had seen Mac glance at his watch the moment he'd moved his hand and she knew that he was silently recording how long this was going to take.

It already seemed to be too long.

'You can do this.' Cade's mouth was right beside Jo's ear. 'I've got you. Take a deep breath and squeeze my hands. And...*push*...'

Jo pushed. And pushed again. She gasped for air and cried out in pain.

'It's coming,' Mac told her. 'You're doing so well, Jo. One more push...'

But Jo was shaking her head and the sound she made was a strangled sob. '... I...*can't*...'

'Yes, you *can*,' Hanna told her fiercely. 'You can do this, Jo. *Push...*'

'I'm here.' Cade's voice was remarkably steady. 'Hold on. Just one more push, baby. *One* more...'

Jo's head was tipped back so that she could see Cade's face and he wasn't breaking the eye contact. Hanna could actually feel the strength that Cade was giving and it was no wonder that she was hanging onto him as if her life depended on it. They were in a world of their own right now and all they could possibly need was each other and Hanna found the tears that had threatened moments ago were now rolling down her cheeks.

And then she realised she'd been wrong. As Mac lifted the baby and Jo and Cade got their first glimpse of their daughter, she knew that they needed this just as much as each other.

Their baby.

Their *family...*

The relief that the baby had been delivered so quickly couldn't be savoured yet. Mac was now completely focused on the physical condition of this infant. Getting her dry was the first priority and he took the soft, clean towel from Hanna to start gently rubbing the pale skin on this tiny body and limbs. He had to ensure the baby didn't lose any body heat and providing stimulation could kick start the signs of life he was desperately looking for.

Was the baby breathing yet? Was her heart rate slow enough to mean she needed CPR? The first APGAR score was needed so that Mac could fill in the paperwork accurately later but, oddly, the criteria and scoring system were a blur in the back of his head as he watched the baby open her eyes and stretch her arms. And then her mouth opened and Mac watched her take her very first breath, pulling the air into her tiny lungs and then scrunching her face into a scowl before letting it out in a scratchy, hiccupping cry that was the best sound Mac had ever heard.

'We should wait at least three minutes to cut the cord,' he said. 'Let's get this little girl skin-to-skin with her mum.'

Cade hadn't moved. He still had Jo in the circle of his arms, his head pressed against hers as Hanna helped shift Jo's remaining clothing and they nestled the baby against her breasts. Mac checked his watch. They'd need to do a five-minute APGAR score at about the same time as cutting the cord. He needed to keep an eye on both the mother and baby until the ambulance arrived but he also needed to find a quiet spot and use his phone to dictate everything he could remember about this birth for the medical records. Lists of what he needed to monitor and warning signs to keep a watch for, like any post-partum bleeding from Jo, were crystal clear in his head now, thank goodness. He could tick them off and stay on top of this situation without being ambushed or distracted by the kind of emotions he could feel swirling around him.

Even Hanna being a complete puddle wasn't surprising. Jo was her best friend and Mac hadn't realised quite how high risk this pregnancy had been. Or that it had been a bit of a miracle in the first place. Hanna would be feeling the wash of that relief Mac wasn't allowing himself to indulge in just yet but her expression, as she watched Cade and Jo, oblivious to being observed herself, gave an even more intense impression.

It didn't look like something he would expect to see on the face of someone who'd never wanted to have a baby of her own.

It looked like a longing that was so bone-deep it had been there for ever.

Mac knew what that kind of longing felt like and he wasn't going to step anywhere near that space. It was a decision he'd made a very long time ago and he wasn't about to question the wisdom of something that had served him very well ever since. The sinking sensation of realising that Hanna wanted a very different—incompatible—future from his own, even if she didn't realise it, was something that it would be irresponsible to ignore.

He got to his feet. Both Jo and the baby were in great hands being monitored by Cade and Hanna.

'I think I can hear a siren,' Mac said. 'I'll go out to the road and flag them down.'

CHAPTER TEN

IT CAME IN WAVES.

Hanna could feel them, taking turns, washing her in one direction and then the completely opposite direction, over the next few days. Like a tide going in and out with no prospect of it stopping anytime soon.

At one end of what was becoming an unwelcome emotional spectrum were the beliefs that had underpinned her choices ever since she'd become an adult. She wasn't going to let the fact that she couldn't have children detract from living life to the full. It could be seen as a blessing, in fact, because it gave her no distraction from giving everything she had to a career she loved, the freedom to travel anywhere she desired, and the independence to live where and how she wanted.

Not that she wanted to continue her current living situation, she told Jo, when she was having a hands-free chat on her phone as she drove to work to start a night shift in the emergency department.

'I actually got up this morning to find a strange, *naked* man standing in the kitchen.'

'No way...' But Jo sounded amused. 'What was he doing?'

'Making coffee.'

'Mmm...coffee. I need some. Stat.'

'Not enough sleep again last night?'

'Almost none. Our daughter might be small but she's mighty. Mighty hungry, anyway.'

'Have you decided on her name?'

'Yes. Olioli. It means joy in Samoan. We'll just call her Oli, though.'

'Oh, nice... I love it.' Hanna was smiling as she turned into Princess Margaret's staff car park. 'It's perfect.'

She could feel flashes of the joy that had come from the dramatic but fortunately safe arrival of this special baby amidst the chaos of the first few days of her friends becoming parents a little earlier than expected.

She could also feel the shock of realising that she might have been totally wrong for her entire adult life. That her conviction that she was never going to miss being able to have children herself had just been exposed as the biggest lie ever. Had she really brushed off Jo's determination to have a baby before it was too late by emphatically saying 'rather you than me'? She completely understood that longing to be a mother now. Because it was eating a hole in her heart at the other end of that emotional spectrum. Maybe it was more like a pendulum than a tide, Hanna thought. She was swinging from one side to the other and it was making her feel a little sick.

Jo's voice broke into her thoughts. 'We've made another decision too.'

'What's that?'

'I'm not going to go back to work full time after my maternity leave. These early years with Oli are too important.'

Hanna could understand that, too. How hard would it be to balance a full-on career with how much you wanted to be the one to care for your precious baby?

'So I'm going to resign,' Jo added. 'Hey… You should tell Mac. Maybe he'd like to apply for the permanent position?'

Hanna laughed. 'I doubt it. He's an international figure. Why would he want to move to a tiny city at the bottom of the world?'

the last few days because he'd started covering some night shifts before Hanna was rostered for any. Today was the first time their work hours—and by default their hours off—would match since the day that Oli had arrived. Since that pendulum had started swinging.

'Sounds like you're needed,' she told Jo, reaching for the button to end the call. 'And it's time I got to work.'

Hanna Peterson was the first person Mac saw in the department when he arrived to do his last rostered night shift. He only saw her back as she pushed a trolley into an examination room but there was no mistaking that long braid hanging down the centre of her back. Hair the colour of flames and as soft as silk. As unique as Hanna's hazel green eyes that had caught his attention so emphatically that first day in Prague. Eyes that should have come with a warning that they belonged to the most captivating woman he was ever going to meet.

The woman who was perfect for him in every way except for one thing that he hadn't seen coming. He'd wondered, later that night, if he simply imagined what he'd seen in Hanna's face when she was holding that newborn baby, but he'd had too much time, in the last few long night shifts and the days where sleep had been hard to catch, to unpick everything that he'd seen and, more importantly, felt that night.

And, because their shift hours meant they hadn't been able to share more than a text conversation or two, he hadn't been completely distracted by being physically close to Hanna, either. He hadn't been able to smell the fragrance of that gorgeous hair. Or feel the silk of her skin. He hadn't been ambushed by the overwhelming desire to sink into the astonishing intimacy they always seemed to find so effortlessly, which automatically seemed to disarm any warning signals and stifle any doubts.

In some ways it would be preferable to ignore what he'd seen. To keep enjoying his time with Hanna here in New Zealand. To let himself dream that they could come up with a plan that would mean it didn't actually have to end at all...

But his new knowledge, that had come straight out of left field, was too big to ignore. Too important, because it changed everything. Ironically, they'd actually discussed it that day in the forest.

You can't change how you feel about something that big because someone else wants you to...

He'd tried to argue with himself about that. He'd wondered if he could change *his* mind about wanting children himself, but he could hear the echoes of his own voice.

If you have to change that much to try and make a relationship work, it's doomed anyway.

It didn't matter how often he went over and over it all in his head, approaching it from every direction. There was no getting away from the clincher.

It might not have felt like it, but it would have been far less painful to find that out, make a clean break and move on...

It might be the right thing to do but Mac hadn't come up with an acceptable plan for quite *how* he was going to do it. Somehow, he had to end things without hurting Hanna any more than was inevitable but convincingly enough that she would move on and find someone who could give her so much more than he ever could.

The family she might not even realise how much she actually wanted.

He was still watching the woman he was going to have to walk away from, even though it was the last thing he *wanted* to do. The last thing a big part of him wanted to do, anyway. There was another part that was going to be relieved, of course. The part that embraced control and made careful plans and checklists. The part that kept him on track and maintained those careful boundaries in his personal life that he'd strayed too far past recently.

The part of Mac that had kept him safe for so long now. After that disastrous slip up in his youth where he'd been prepared to discard his life plan for the woman he'd loved and the baby that would give him another chance of having a family, only to have it all ripped away from him, he'd never let his control slip.

Was what he knew now perhaps his version of a 'get out of jail free' card?

Hanna had vanished into the examination room and that was a reminder that it was time to push any personal issues completely out of sight while he did his job. It helped that the part of his brain that kept those lists

and that control in his personal life also provided the distance that enabled him to keep
sight of a bigger picture when it came to
diagnosing and treating patients within the
framework of keeping an entire emergency
department running smoothly.

It did run smoothly, in both a personal
and professional sense, until the early morning hours of that night shift, when he saw
Hanna coming through a cubicle curtain,
with a baby in her arms, a concerned frown
on her face. An older woman, behind her,
had red eyes as if she'd been crying and a
handful of tissues pressed to her face as she
blew her nose.

Mac could feel his control slip a notch.
Because this was Hanna. Because she was
holding a baby, which tapped into everything
he'd been thinking about so much. Because
seeing her look so concerned made him want
to step in instantly and help. But this wasn't
about Hanna. Or himself. It was about a very
vulnerable small person who'd been brought
into the emergency department.

Instantly using the assessment tool of the
paediatric triangle was as automatic as taking his next breath. Within taking a couple
of steps closer, Mac was not alarmed by the

general appearance of this baby and couldn't
see any obvious signs of poor circulation like
mottled hands or a blueish tinge to the face.
He could, however, hear the sounds of a baby
who was in respiratory distress with overly
rapid breathing and audible wheezing. And
he would never forget the golden rule that
adequate evaluation was impossible if a child
was fully clothed.

'Follow me,' he directed. 'Resus One's
free. What's going on?'

'His grandma's just brought him in because
he wasn't feeding properly and wouldn't set-
tle. He's not running a temperature and hasn't
got a runny nose, but she noticed a sudden
onset of wheezing and his breathing's got noticeably worse in the few minutes I've been
with them.'

Mac let Hanna go ahead as he spoke to
the woman following her. 'Any chance that
baby's inhaled or choked on anything?'

'I don't think so.' The woman shook her
head. 'Except he did seem to be having trouble swallowing his milk an hour or so ago.
That was when he started coughing and I
thought his breathing didn't sound quite
right.'

'Has he been unwell in any other way before this?'

'No… A bit unsettled, maybe, but he has been, right from the start. And he's never been a good sleeper. That's why I told my daughter and son-in-law I'd take him for the night—so they could get a decent sleep themselves.'

'How old is he?'

'Four months. His name's Taika.'

Hanna was gently putting the baby down on the bed in the middle of the room. She began unbuttoning the stretchy sleep suit he was wearing, distracting and soothing him with a constant singsong explanation of what she was doing.

Mac was fitting his stethoscope to his ears.

'Any family history of allergies or asthma?'

'I'm not sure.'

Mac froze, blinking slowly. 'Sorry?'

'Taika's adopted,' she said. 'Sorry, I should have told you this before, shouldn't I? I do actually forget sometimes. He's such a wanted baby and he couldn't be loved any more—by any of us. Oh, my…' She was reaching for her tissues again. 'I didn't want to wake them up before I had to but I should ring them now, shouldn't I?'

Baby Taika began crying as Mac approached with his stethoscope, which wasn't a bad thing when assessing a baby's appearance or reactions but it made it impossible to auscultate a chest effectively. Hanna picked him up and held him against her shoulder with one hand cradling his head and he settled enough for Mac to listen to some worrying lung sounds, with the possible causes and more questions that needed answering lining up in his head.

Was this a case of a viral illness like bronchiolitis or RSV even though he wasn't yet showing other symptoms of a respiratory infection? Was it an allergic reaction that might lead to his condition deteriorating rapidly? Or was it an aspiration pneumonia from milk or a foreign object? The wheeze that was getting louder suggested obstructive pathology and a chest X-ray was high on the list for investigations to rule out something caught in tiny airways.

There was another reason to take an X-ray that became apparent as Hanna put the baby down again so that he could look for other indications of respiratory distress like the retraction of the muscles between ribs.

Bruises.

Just faint marks on his ribs but Mac's focus narrowed sharply as another automatic thought process was triggered by a solidly embedded alarm system.

If they can't cruise, they can't bruise...

He couldn't let that alarm bell sound so loudly it drowned anything else out, however. Tunnel vision, thanks to one sign or symptom standing out enough to disguise others, was a trap for the unwary. Mac always had mental checklists available to cover possibilities for a differential diagnosis and he wasn't about to jump to any conclusions.

But Hanna had noticed the bruises as well. She only caught his gaze for a heartbeat but he couldn't miss the sudden change in the atmosphere in this room as Mac felt a nasty knot forming in his gut. Was she thinking the same thing he was—that Taika's grandmother had potentially given them cause to be on alert by saying that his parents were suffering from sleep deprivation? That this baby was not their biological child?

When the X-ray images were available a

short time later, that knot in Mac's gut expanded so fast he actually felt sick.

'There,' he said quietly, his finger on the screen as Hanna looked over his shoulder. 'And there...'

'Oh, my God,' Hanna breathed. 'Those marks are all *fractures*?'

'Very recent ones,' Mac said grimly. 'On both the clavicle and these ribs. It could well be the reason his breathing is affected.'

'But his grandmother's so involved with his care and she obviously loves Taika. She says her daughter, Gemma, is finding things tough but she adores her son. She's apparently worried sick. She's on her way here now.' Hanna was biting her lip. 'Do we need to bring Social Services in?'

'Not just yet.' Mac took a slow breath in. There were steps to this process. A case of child abuse couldn't be allowed to slip through but, on the other hand, a mistaken accusation was also unacceptable. 'I'd like to do a much more thorough physical assessment. But we'll get some more images done. Of his long bones and spine.'

'To look for other fractures?'

Mac nodded. 'But also to look for any evidence of underlying bone disease. I can't see any beading on the ribs in these images, but it's quite possible to have a mild form of osteogenesis imperfecta that won't be that easy to diagnose. It's a shame we can't find out if there's any family history of scoliosis or fractures or dislocations, but we might see thinning of the long bones if there is inherited disease. There are other investigations that can be done like skin and bone biopsies. We'll keep Taika in, and I'll get a specialist orthopaedic consult booked as early as possible in the morning. I need to talk to his parents, too.' His heart was sinking even further at the thought of a conversation that could be distressing for everybody involved. 'It's going to be a long night, I think.'

The case of baby Taika cast a pall over the rest of the night shift, especially after his parents arrived and were so clearly shocked to be faced with what had already been discovered about their son's condition. Hanna spent much of her time with the family and watched their care of the baby as he was treated with pain relief for his fractures and oxygen along with an inhaler for his breathing. She became more and more convinced that this wasn't a case of a child who was being abused.

She completely understood why Mac was being so thorough, however. This was beyond important to him. Hanna only had to remember that opening address he'd given at the Prague conference to be reminded of that little boy who thought an emergency department was his 'safe' space. She'd told him how heartbreaking the story had been and how much she had wanted to cuddle that little boy herself but there was nothing about Taika that struck the same kind of chord. Her instincts told her that he was a longed-for and much-loved baby.

'They're beside themselves with worry,' she said to Mac as their shift was finally ending. 'How long will it be until they get some answers?'

'I've spoken to the paediatric orthopaedic guy who will be reviewing the initial X-rays. He's going to meet the family at nine o'clock and he'll call in anyone else he deems necessary.' Mac glanced at his watch. 'I might hang around and see what he has to say.'

'That's two hours away.' Hanna looked at the deep creases around Mac's eyes. She knew how tired he had to be, but she could also sense how tightly strung he was. 'I don't suppose you're going to try and catch some sleep first?'

Mac simply shook his head. 'I'll go and find some coffee. Take a walk, maybe. It should be getting light outside soon.'

'Want some company?'

Another shake of his head was accompanied by a smile this time. 'You need to sleep.'

'Not going to happen,' Hanna said quietly. 'Not when I'm worried about you.'

The beat of silence that fell between them made it feel as if she'd just told Mac exactly how she felt about him and, in a way, she had. She'd let him know that his wellbeing was just as important, if not more so, than her own.

The hesitation before he caught her gaze was telling. A hollow feeling inside Hanna's chest was expanding to the point where it was difficult to take a breath and it only got worse when Mac spoke.

'Okay…come for a walk with me,' he said. 'It's been a while since we've had a chance to talk properly.'

His gaze slid away from Hanna's as he spoke and she was aware of a heaviness— as though there was too much air inside that hollow space. People usually only said they wanted to 'talk' when they had something to say that the other person was not going to like. Chillingly, this took her back to that moment in the park in Barcelona, after that amazing dance under the tree, when she had sensed that the heat of the passion they'd discovered was burning itself out and Mac was either pulling away or putting some kind of barrier in place.

That, for whatever reason—probably because there was too much emotion involved—he needed to escape into his safe, buttoned-up space where everything was under control.

Hanna swallowed hard. Something had changed for Mac as well, hadn't it? But when? Had it been the birth of Oli, as it had been for her, or was it the case of baby Taika tonight that had got under his skin so much? Whatever it was, Hanna knew that it was going to affect her as well.

'Where would you like to go for a walk?'

Mac shrugged. 'Doesn't matter. You choose.'

Hanna could feel the chill of the frosty dawn approaching as they walked outside. It did matter, she thought. This might be one of the most significant decisions she'd made in a long time.

* * *

'Where are we?'

'A special place,' Hanna told him. 'Tunnel Beach.'

The idea of bringing Mac here had occurred to Hanna the moment she'd turned out of the hospital car park, knowing they had a couple of hours up their sleeves. This was where she had come to take part in a very significant event not so long ago when she'd been the bridesmaid for her best friend. Given the even more significant event of the birth of their child that both she and Mac had been a part of, it seemed exactly the place they needed to be.

'I can't see the beach.' Mac turned his head as he looked through the windscreen. 'But it looks like the apocalypse is about to happen.'

Dramatic blood red and tangerine orange streaks outlined their uninterrupted view of the horizon above a still inky black ocean.

Hanna grinned. 'I was hoping it was going to be a stunning sunrise. They often are with a frosty start to the day. And it's kind of a secret beach,' she added. 'It's where Jo and Cade got married. Where they had their first date, in fact. You have to climb down steps through a tunnel, which probably isn't the best idea while it's still dark, but we can watch the sunrise and then have a walk if you don't mind getting cold.'

'It would certainly keep me awake.'

'I don't think you need anything more to keep you awake, do you?'

It wasn't just the deep crinkles around Mac's eyes, or the dark shadows beneath him. Hanna could feel how tense he was and the need to offer him comfort or support or whatever it was that he needed was a glow as strong as the sunrise unfolding in front of them. She reached to touch his face softly with her fingertips and, when he turned and smiled at her, she felt a little piece of her heart crack.

'What is it?' she whispered. 'Is this about Taika? About his injuries? Or is it because he's adopted that makes you feel so involved?'

Mac looked away. He let his eyes drift shut. 'Both,' he admitted quietly.

Hanna stared at him. She couldn't say anything. She could feel the silence in the car folding in on her as she realised what had been there in front of her all along. Hidden in plain sight.

'Oh, my God.' Her voice shook. 'That little boy in your story…who only felt cared for when he was being taken care of in hospital… It was *you*, wasn't it?'

Mac didn't say anything. He didn't need to. Or maybe he guessed that Hanna was shocked enough to need a moment to process things.

So much was suddenly making sense to her. Like why Mac was so buttoned up. That being so organised and predictable and never putting a foot out of place might have been the only way to try and keep himself safe as a child. That the need to protect his own unborn child must have been overwhelming and to be told that baby no longer existed would have seemed like the ultimate failure when he'd been determined to take responsibility.

No wonder this man had never simply followed his nose to find an adventure. Or let himself get close enough to anyone to contemplate marriage or the responsibilities of bringing children into the world. Why would anyone make themselves vulnerable to yet another instance of being abused? Letting themselves feel unwanted. Rejected.

Unloved…

That crack in her heart was growing into a full-on break. Like the way she'd wanted to cuddle that little boy in his story, all Hanna wanted to do was to gather Mac into her arms and hold him tight.

To let him know how much he was loved.

But that would be the worst thing she could do, wouldn't it?

Deep inside this intelligent, skilled, perceptive and sensitive man, who had a wonderful sense of humour and the ability to be the most generous lover ever, was a small boy. One who'd been hurt often enough to learn not to trust the people who should have loved him. Who might have even *said* that they loved him but acted very, very differently. And there was a young man, about to grasp the freedom of making his own choices and willingly stepping up to make sure his own child didn't feel unwanted or unloved, who'd been hurt again, so badly he'd chosen to travel alone through life.

She'd known she couldn't ask for his trust or a commitment of any kind. He had to be the one to offer it. Right now, it felt like he was moving further away from her rather than closer and it also felt like there was nothing she could do about it. If she went after him, in an emotional sense, she knew he would only run faster. Because that was the only way he could feel safe? If she stayed very still, maybe he would slow down enough to think about things. Perhaps, if he was allowed to choose himself, he might turn around and come back?

Even the spectacular sunrise was fading in front of them now.

It was Mac who broke the silence in the end. 'It's ancient history,' he said. 'But you're the only person I've ever talked to about it.'

Hanna swallowed carefully. 'Thank you,' she said softly. She waited until he turned his head to meet her gaze and then she waited for another heartbeat, just to hold his gaze. To try and tell him what she couldn't say aloud.

'What for?'

It felt like Mac was holding onto her gaze as if he was searching for something. He had that focused, narrow-eyed expression that told Hanna she was the only thing that mattered in that moment.

She loved that.

It felt like love, even if Mac still couldn't let himself admit it.

Hanna smiled at him. 'For trusting me...'

She broke the eye contact, before the moment could get any heavier, by looking out of the window. 'It's light enough to be safe to walk along the top of a cliff,' she said. 'We could even go down the tunnel.'

Mac checked his watch. 'Maybe we should head back. I'd hate to miss that meeting. We could come back another day?'

'We could…'

Hanna was smiling as she started the car again. Because this way, it was easy to do that standing still thing and not push Mac somewhere he wasn't ready to go. And 'another day' suggested he wasn't going to run too far, too soon.

It was a reprieve.

Wrapped up in hope…

CHAPTER ELEVEN

FINDING WHAT FELT like a justifiable reason to avoid doing something difficult or unpleasant—like telling someone that a relationship couldn't continue—made it easier to continue doing it.

It also felt like a much kinder option and there was no one else on earth that Mac would want to be kind to more than Hanna Peterson.

Fate was also lending a helping hand. Jo's decision not to return to work full time after her maternity leave led to an almost instant offer of a permanent position for Mac, apparently due to the glowing reports of the time he had already spent in the Princess Margaret's emergency department.

'I can't take it, of course,' Mac told Hanna that evening, when they found time to be together in Jo's little house, relaxing on the couch in front of the fire. 'I've got far too many commitments, including a job in Edinburgh and research projects I'm involved with in Europe and the States. I've loved being here but it was never going to be for ever.'

'I know…' Hanna snuggled in under his arm to tuck her head against his chest. 'I doubt anyone expected the world-famous Dr MacMillan to emigrate to a wee town at the bottom of the world. We're lucky you decided to come for a busman's holiday.'

That summed it up nicely, didn't it? Doing his real job but in a very different location. That blurred space between a holiday and real life. Like the space between a relationship and a holiday fling that he and Hanna had claimed as their own. Neither could work on a permanent basis, however, despite any plans they might play with to meet up again on holiday. Mac doubted that Hanna expected that to work, either. They would drift apart as their real lives took over. Hanna would meet someone else. Someone who could give her far more than Mac could.

He bent his head, placing a kiss on Hanna's hair.

'Did you know that Jo dropped by to give me a heads-up that the position was going to be advertised so it could well impact the length of my locum? I suspect it was because of her that I got approached directly.'

'You're her favourite person right now. You played a big part in Oli's safe arrival.'

'She had Oli with her. It's a great name, isn't it?'

'The full version is Olioli. It means "joy" in Samoan.'

Mac nodded. 'So Jo told me. The name suits her. She was spreading joy right through the department. Or maybe it was because Jo's looking so extraordinarily happy.' He reached for the glass of wine on the low table beside the couch. 'She also told me that she's planning to sell this house. She's hoping you'll buy it.'

'I'm seriously thinking about it.' Hanna seemed to be watching the flames in the gas fire that was flickering in front of them. 'I'm kind of over having flatmates. I think it's time I grew up and settled down.'

'I can't imagine you settled down,' Mac murmured. 'I'll always see you as a free spirit, following your nose and finding amazing adventures.'

It was only a heartbeat of silence but it felt…odd. As if he wasn't the only one who was avoiding saying something difficult? Mac felt the need to break it.

'I forgot to tell you. The results on Taika's bone biopsy came through today. You were right. There's a reason for his fractures that has nothing to do with abuse.'

Hanna lifted her head. 'It *is* osteogenesis imperfecta?'

'Yes.'

'Oh…his parents must be devastated.'

'It's Type One, which is mild. And there are treatments available now, like cyclic infusions of different drugs that can reduce incidence of fractures and increase bone density. The whole family is completely focused on whatever needs to be done to help.'

'I knew they loved him.' Hanna's eyes had the kind of shimmer that advertised imminent tears. 'His parents had wanted a baby for *so* long…'

'He's a lucky little boy,' Mac agreed.

One of those tears escaped Hanna's eyes as she leaned against him again. 'I hate that you weren't so lucky, Mac,' she whispered.

It was another one of those silences, but Mac couldn't think of anything to say.

'Maybe your sister was one of the lucky ones, too,' Hanna said. 'I know it's tragic that she died so young but maybe she had parents who adored her. A grandma, even, like Taika?'

Mac shrugged. 'Guess I'll never know.' He placed another kiss on the top of Hanna's head. 'It's getting late. Come to bed with me?'

But Hanna ignored the suggestion. 'Where did she grow up?' she asked. 'Didn't you want to know what that was like for her to live in New Zealand?'

'I checked a map before I came. Dunedin's close enough.'

'To where?'

'Oamaru.'

'That's where she lived? Oh…that *is* close,' Hanna exclaimed. 'It would be so easy to go and have a look. It's only a bit over an hour's drive away. I've been through it often enough but I've never stopped to really explore it. And, hey…we've both got a day off tomorrow…'

Mac stood up. He held out his hand, knowing that Hanna would take it and he could pull her to her feet. It would only take another tug and she would be in his arms and he could kiss her lips instead of her hair and they would be upstairs and in bed very, very soon and he wouldn't have to come up with a reason why he didn't want to go and see exactly where his sister had grown up. He didn't need another link to this country that would make it any more difficult to leave.

But he could see a glow in Hanna's eyes that he'd seen before. That excitement that she could find in throwing caution to the winds and following her nose. Or her heart.

'There's so many things I could show you. We could go the scenic route into Central Otago and up through Danseys Pass. I've heard about a famous old hotel at the top but I've never found the time to go there. It's been a long time since we had an adventure.'

She stood on her tiptoes and kissed Mac on his lips and it reminded him of the way she had said goodbye that first day they'd met before she ran back towards the hotel. They would be saying goodbye again, possibly sooner than he'd expected and Mac knew how much he was going to miss Hanna. He also knew how unlikely it was that he would ever do something truly impulsive again without her encouragement.

And that sparked another memory. Of something Hanna had said in front of that same clock.

'We've got time now... Let's not waste a minute of it...'

It wasn't that he couldn't say 'no' to her.

He just didn't want to. Perhaps because he wanted to make the most of every minute he still had to spend with Hanna?'

'So...this road is called the Pigroot.' Hanna's sporty little Mini was eating up the miles of the road heading into Central Otago after they'd turned off the coastal road north of Dunedin.

'Hmm...' Mac had his phone out already. 'According to this, we're on State Highway 85.'

'Technically, that would be correct,' Hanna agreed.

'It says that we're going through some of the most historic gold mining territory in New Zealand.'

'Most of Central Otago was gold mining country.'

'It also says that the Maniototo plain has the most extreme climate in New Zealand. Well below zero in winter and over thirty degrees Celsius in summer.'

'That would explain why my gran used to take me to Naseby to go ice-skating when

I was a kid. She was the one who told me it was called the Pigroot. She just didn't tell me why.' Hanna cast a sideways glance at Mac, who was so focused on the information he was taking in that it wouldn't have surprised her if he started taking notes. Or making a list of everything he wanted to see.

She loved that about him. His curiosity and attention to detail. His focus…especially when it was on herself. It was one of the first things she'd noticed about him, in fact—the way his eyes narrowed and the creases appeared as his attention was caught. Not that it stopped him from still being aware of the big picture and was that part of why he was travelling alone in life—that ability to consider consequences of all sorts of possibilities? As always, the thought that Mac had been lonely in the past or could be in the future gave her heart a painful squeeze.

He didn't need to be. She would be happy to be with him for the rest of her life. So happy…

'Okay…there are different stories about how the road got its name.' Mac put his phone away. 'The winner seems to be that the local wild pigs were so friendly that they'd come and rub their noses with any travellers' horses.'

'I like that.' Hanna smiled. 'Friendly locals. We're coming into Naseby now and I'd love to see the lake where I used to go skating but, if you're not too hungry yet, it might be better to wait till we get up the Danseys Pass to get lunch.'

The wild, winding gravel and sand road of the pass cut through the tussock-covered land of high-country farms with snow-dusted mountain views at every turn. The long, low stone building of the hotel blended into the landscape and offered the perfect place to take a break. There was a roaring open fire heating the interior, with a display of antique bottles on the mantelpiece. Bleached deer antlers hung on the wall near the table that Hanna and Mac chose and the beer-battered fish and chips they both ordered for lunch were delicious.

'I used to ice-skate when I was a kid, too,' Mac told her. 'That lake in Naseby reminds me of the one we had on our property.'

'You had a *lake*?' Hanna's jaw dropped.

'Still do. Not that I've skated on it in the last thirty years or more. The estate's a fair way out of Edinburgh so it was easier to get a manager in and live near the hospital.' Mac shook his head. 'I've been putting off deciding what to do with it but I think it's time to sell up. I'll never live there again. It's far too big for one person.'

'Sounds like a castle.'

'More of a manor house but the villagers used to call me the "kid from the castle". It was probably a good thing I got sent to boarding schools from an early age because no one from the village wanted to have anything to do with me.'

Hanna made a small sound of agreement. It would have saved Mac from more than simply being bullied by other children but how lonely had it been?

'I think I will buy Jo's house,' she said quietly. 'It's a perfect size for me.' As a bonus, it would also be filled with memories of being there with Mac. She put down her fork. 'Do you ever worry about getting older?' she asked. 'And still being alone?'

Mac shook his head. 'I'm used to it,' was all he said.

He turned to glance at people settling at a nearby table. A highchair was being found for a baby who looked to be about six months old. A little girl who dropped her toy and began crying as she was put into the chair. Her father retrieved the fluffy rabbit and made it pop up from beneath the tray of the chair and the baby's cry changed to a gurgle of laughter.

Hanna was also watching them, smiling at the sound of the baby's laugh. That would be Jo and Cade in a few months' time, she thought. Out together as a family.

Never alone.

She put down her cutlery moments later, her appetite fading. She'd been used to being alone, too, especially when she'd gone travelling but there was no appeal to be found in doing it again. After being with Mac in Barcelona, she'd felt so alone as she went on to Corsica and then Italy. Things that she would have previously revelled in—like a stunning sunset on the Amalfi Coast—felt so diminished by not having someone to share it with that it might as well have never happened.

Okay…by not having Mac to share it with.

Another peal of laughter from the baby made Hanna smile again but she was suddenly aware of Mac's gaze focused on her. She turned to find an intensity in that gaze that made her catch her breath.

He knew, didn't he? He knew about the longing deep within that had been born at the same time as Oli. Not simply changing her mind about wanting a child but the need for a whole family of her own.

That smile…

Mac loved that smile.

The joy that Hanna was getting from just observing someone else's child made Mac remember the way she'd looked the night that Jo and Cade's baby was born and she'd held that tiny person in her own arms.

That thought morphed into his body reminding him of what it felt like when *he* was in her arms. And the way he'd felt that day on the bus trip when she'd taken hold of his hand and…and he hadn't felt alone…

Hanna had so much love to give. She was the warmest, bravest, most generous person he'd ever met and he loved that about her.

No…

He loved *her*. Not just her different attributes but the whole of Hanna. He was *in* love with her. He couldn't imagine willingly walking away from her, in fact. How could he go back to his old life and be an entire world away from her?

He could change his life, though, couldn't he?

It was the baby's laughter behind him that

sparked the moment that fear stepped in. A reminder of why he couldn't change his life that much. Why he couldn't allow himself to step into the vulnerability of loving anyone like this. Giving them the power to affect every decision you made for the future.

Losing control...

That fear was always there, wasn't it? Buried for so long now but it would never go away completely. Even as a child he'd known that control was the key. If everything was in its place and doing what it was supposed to do—like the intricate workings inside a clock—it was less likely that something bad would happen.

Something that could hurt in ways that cut far deeper than anything purely physical.

Was it his imagination or could he see a reflection of what he was feeling in Hanna's eyes? A flicker of that fear? He broke the eye contact before she could sense any more of what he was thinking.

He managed to find a smile. 'Cute baby.'

'Shall we go?' Hanna's tone held a note of forced brightness. 'We don't want to run out of time.'

Mac paid the bill and followed Hanna outside. 'Would you like me to drive? So you can enjoy the scenery more?'

'Sure.' Hanna handed over the keys. 'You can't go wrong for directions. We just follow this road until we get to the end and turn right to go to the coast.'

She was quiet as they drove further through the pass and Mac could feel a tension between them that had never been there before. A tension that he didn't like one little bit but what could he do to get rid of it? Having to concentrate on his driving wasn't helping. He had to go slowly around bends knowing that there would not be enough room if they met a campervan or a farm vehicle coming the other way and there was an alarming drop to one side into a gorge with a river at the bottom.

When he saw an intersection with another road ahead of them, he slowed to peer at the signpost.

'Island Cliff Road.'

'We need to keep going,' Hanna said. 'We haven't got to Duntroon yet.'

But this road looked as if it went somewhere. It was sealed, at least at this point, and it was wide enough to have a white line in the middle.

Mac lifted an eyebrow. 'How 'bout we follow our noses instead? I've heard that you find the best adventures that way.'

At last, the tension seemed to be receding. A slow smile curved Hanna's lips and reached as far as her eyes. He held the direct gaze and could actually feel the love that was there, just for him, as if it was a three-dimensional gift. Or maybe a four-dimensional one given that there was no time limit?

Except there kind of was.

Hanna might have said that they didn't want to run out of time but, really, they had no choice, did they? Time was running out on them and maybe that had been the root cause of that tension. They both knew that this was nearly over.

Perhaps that had something to do with the fact that Mac was driving a lot faster on this sealed road that led to who knew where? Maybe the steepness of the hill was contributing as well, along with the curve in the road that was deep enough to conceal the approach of a large milk tanker.

Mac thought he had enough room to get out of the way. What he didn't factor in, as the truck roared past and kept going, were the shingle verges of this rural road and how you could lose all control of your vehicle when the tyres hit the loose material. He did know the moment he lost control of this little car, however. He could feel it sliding.

Spinning.

Bouncing off the road and taking out a post and wire fence before the passenger side of the car came to a sickening, bone-jolting crunching halt against a massive rock the size of a small hill.

There was only one thing Mac was aware of in the moment the airbags exploded around them.

Fear.

Had he hurt Hanna?

This fear was bigger than anything he'd ever felt before. Darker. It had the potential to be the forerunner of something utterly soul-destroying.

Had he *killed* Hanna?

The fear grew into horror as he turned his head to see her head slumped sideways, her eyes closed, her skin so pale it looked like every freckle had been painted on by hand.

'Oh, my God…' The words were torn out of Mac. *'Hanna…'*

CHAPTER TWELVE

HER EYES OPENED as she heard his voice.

Or maybe it was the touch of his fingers on her cheek. Hardly the best medical practice to check to see if someone was still breathing or had a pulse but the need to make physical contact was driven by emotions, not logic.

Mac had seen these eyes countless times now. He was intimately familiar with that tawny, auburn shade that was an exact match to her hair, around the blackness of her pupils, with its sunburst rays going into the mix of green and gold that became hazel. A unique, wild combination of colours and shapes that were neatly contained by rims as dark as their centres.

He'd seen these eyes glow with the excitement of a new adventure, soften with tenderness and sparkle with tears when she was moved. They were her emotional barometers. The windows to her soul. He'd seen them flicker with fear only recently and he knew she might see far more than that in his own eyes right now.

The fear that he might have lost her for ever. Mac hadn't cried since he'd been a very young child but he could feel the prickle of tears forming behind his eyes now as he watched Hanna open hers. Because for a tiny moment in time, she looked dazed as she stared back at him. Blank. He could see the moment they began to focus but he could *feel* the moment she recognised him and he knew he was lost.

He could never walk away from this woman.

She hadn't simply taken a place in his heart.

She *was* his heart.

It only took a heartbeat. A moment suspended in time that vanished as soon as Hanna blinked.

'Don't move,' he told her. 'Just tell me if anything hurts.'

Hanna blinked again and then gave her head a tiny shake as she lifted it. 'I'm okay…'

'Don't move your neck,' Mac ordered. 'Try and take a deep breath.'

Hanna did draw in a deep breath, but she was ignoring the direction to stay still as she sat up straighter. 'Honestly... I'm fine. Nothing hurts. Are *you* all right?'

'I'm fine. It wasn't my side of the car that hit the rock. But you were knocked out. Can you remember what day it is? Where we are?'

'I have no idea where we are exactly. We were following *your* nose, remember?' Hanna unclipped her safety belt. 'And I didn't get knocked out. I was just a bit dazed by that bump. And the fright of those airbags going off like bombs. I remember everything. That milk tanker. Skidding in the gravel. Going through the fence. I could see the rock.'

Mac could see it now, through the broken window on Hanna's side of the car.

'It was my fault,' he said. 'Oh, God, Hanna. I'm so sorry.'

'Don't be daft,' Hanna said. 'That truck was going far too fast around that bend. His wheels were way over the centre line. You managed to avoid a head-on collision that would have killed us both.'

Amazingly, there was a smile on Hanna's face now. And a softness in her eyes that

Mac had seen before but not in broad daylight like this. It made him think of those moments he held her in his arms when they'd finally finished making love. When they were drifting in that space between ecstasy and reality that only existed because they were together. Time that had a dreamlike quality that almost made you believe in magic.

Except...was that sparkle in Hanna's eyes now due to tears?

No. She was still smiling.

'You're my hero,' she said, her voice wobbling. 'I love you, Mac.'

And there it was.

It had been there all along, hadn't it? The words were forming themselves in his head and escaping and it felt like the moment the car's tyres had hit gravel and he'd lost any control of its trajectory.

'I love you, too, Hanna,' he said softly. 'I think I always have. I know I always will.'

Sitting in a crumpled car in a paddock with huge rocks in the middle of nowhere shouldn't have been a romantic setting.

But it was.

It was the most romantic moment in

Hanna Peterson's life and it wouldn't have mattered where they were or what was—or had been—happening around them. Because Mac loved her. He was *in* love with her and, most significantly, he knew he was.

He'd said the words aloud. And then he'd kissed her as if nothing else on earth mattered but to hold her face between his hands and touch her lips with his own so tenderly it was heartbreaking enough that Hanna suspected they weren't simply her own tears causing the dampness on her cheeks.

And Mac knew she felt the same way and it wasn't scaring him off despite any fear of letting someone close enough to create a vulnerability he'd spent his life trying to avoid. If anything, any vestige of barriers between them had been completely removed. That focused look of his as he watched her for any signs of being in pain was sharper than ever before, as if his gaze was completely unguarded. Even the touch of his hands, as he helped Hanna climb out of the driver's side of the Mini because the passenger door was crumpled enough to have jammed, felt different.

Protective.

It felt like a promise, even, that it would

always be there to support her if she should need it. Something that she could trust. When she put her feet on the grass outside the car and Mac pulled her to her feet and straight into his arms to hold her close to his body it felt like the place she would always be waiting to get back to.

It felt like home.

But this was not the time to sink into the bliss of that feeling. There were things that needed to be done. They couldn't stay standing in some farmer's paddock when any real warmth from winter sunshine would soon be fading as the afternoon wore on.

'Oh, help...' Hanna pulled back from Mac's arms. 'I hope this isn't a sheep paddock. With that hole in the fence, we'll have to try and stop them getting out onto the road.'

'We need help,' Mac decided, looking around. 'I can't see any sheep, but I don't think we'll be driving your car anywhere else today.' He pulled out his phone but then frowned at the screen. 'I don't have any reception.'

Hanna reached into the pocket of her jacket. 'I've got one bar. No...that's gone too. Maybe if we get away from these big rocks the signal might be better?'

'Let's walk along the road. If we can't get a signal, we could flag down someone driving past and they might be able to take us to the nearest garage.'

They walked hand in hand. For whatever reason, the traffic appeared to be non-existent at this particular time but that didn't bother Hanna because this still felt like a special bubble of time that they could never have again and she wasn't ready to share it. They walked across short grass between the clumps of tussock in this vast field without feeling the need to talk just yet. There were many decisions that would need to be made but, for now, it was enough to know that they were in love. That they would be sharing those decisions and what was to come.

The rock they'd crashed into wasn't the only protrusion in the landscape around them. There were enormous rocks all over the place. Weird rocks. Huge but almost soft looking. Smooth and rounded like hunched shoulders. They had to stop and simply stare for a while.

'What is this place?' Mac wondered aloud. 'It's extraordinary.'

Hanna stood on tiptoes and put her arms around Mac's neck. 'It's our place,' she whispered. 'Did I tell you that I love you?'

He bent his head to kiss her. Slowly. So, so tenderly. 'I do believe you did.'

He kissed her again. 'And did I tell you I love *you*?'

'You did.' Hanna smiled up at him.

'I thought I'd killed you.' Mac was holding her gaze. 'The accident was my fault, you know. If we'd gone the way you said we should go we'd never have been on that corner when that truck came around.'

'And if we hadn't been, we wouldn't have had that accident.'

'See? I told you it was my fault.'

Hanna ignored him. 'And if we hadn't had that accident you wouldn't have looked at me like that and I might never have been brave enough to tell you that I love you.'

'Why not?'

'Because I didn't think you'd want to hear it. I thought you'd disappear from my life and I didn't want that to happen.'

'I *was* going to leave,' Mac said slowly.

'I know.' Hanna nodded. 'I know you can't stay here. Your home is Scotland. Your work is on the other side of the world.' And she would be happy anywhere as long as she was with Mac.

'That wasn't the reason.'

Hanna caught her breath. She'd known that, too, hadn't she? She'd sensed Mac had been getting ready to leave more than simply a place.

'I saw the way you looked the night that Oli was born. How important having a family was to you even if you didn't realise it. I couldn't give that to you but I wanted you to have the chance to find whatever it is that would make you happy.'

The breath Hanna pulled in was shaky. 'I did realise that it wasn't true that I didn't ever want to have children,' she said quietly. 'But I also realised that I would rather not have children if it meant losing you.'

'I never want to lose you either,' Mac said. 'I only realised how much it mattered when I thought I *had*. But… I don't want you to miss out on something that would make you happy.'

'*You* make me happy.'

'You make me…a different person.' Mac was smiling. 'Someone who can have adventures.'

'Who can dance in a park.' Hanna nodded. 'And follow his nose.'

'Someone who can take risks,' Mac added softly. 'And trust someone else.' He took her hand. 'But only if it's you.'

By tacit consent, they were walking towards the road again. It was time they sorted out the problem with their transport. Finding the reception had improved, Hanna made a call to her roadside assistance service to organise a tow truck.

'No,' she had to tell them. 'I'm not sure exactly where we are. Hang on…' She turned to Mac. 'Can you remember the name of this road?'

'Island Cliff? Wait… There's a sign on the other side of that gate. That might help.' He opened the gate.

'We're at a place called Elephant Rocks,' Hanna was able to tell the roadside rescue call taker a moment later.

'They know exactly where we are,' she told Mac as she ended the call. 'This place is famous. It's even been used in movies.'

'I'm not surprised.' Mac was still on the other side of the gate, reading the sign. 'Those big rocks are limestone outcrops. Twenty-four to twenty-six million years old.'

He was looking impressed. 'Did you know about them?'

'I've never heard of them,' she admitted. 'But you did remind me that following your nose led to the best adventures.'

'We need to go back and have a proper look,' Mac said. 'Apparently you can see remnants of the ancient sea floor in the rocks.' He came back through the gate. 'Do you think we have enough time?'

'The tow truck's coming from Oamaru,' Hanna told him. 'It'll take a while.' Her smile felt misty. 'But you know…we do have the rest of our lives. I reckon that's plenty of time to have adventures, don't you?'

Mac's smile was looking suspiciously misty as well. 'We do. And it is.' He caught her hand. 'But let's not waste a minute of it.'

So, holding hands tightly enough to make it clear that neither of them wanted to let go anytime soon, Hanna and Mac turned back to go and explore Elephant Rocks.

No… Hanna knew it was bigger than that. They were taking the first steps of the best adventure ever. Their future together. She squeezed Mac's hand even tighter.

And he squeezed hers back…

EPILOGUE

Several years later...

THE SMALL WEATHERBOARD house with a riot of colour from the dahlias in the tidy front garden looked exactly the same as it had when they'd parked in front of that picket fence years ago.

'Do you remember that first time?' Hanna asked Mac. 'When we were too scared to get out of the car and go and knock on the front door?'

'How could I forget?' Mac smiled at his wife. 'We had to rent a car to get here to Oamaru because your Mini was still getting repaired. It was never the same after I drove it into that rock, was it?'

'Nothing was ever the same,' Hanna agreed. But she was smiling. 'It was so much better, wasn't it?'

'It was.'

The creases around Mac's eyes deepened. The move he made to lean towards Hanna and the way she met him in the middle to exchange a kiss suggested the ease of something that happened so often it was automatic.

'I did think it might have been a mistake to encourage you to come here, though. We had so much going on already, with planning our wedding and you shifting your whole life to New Zealand. There was no way to know whether raking up the past would turn out to be a blessing or a complete disaster.'

The small whimper from the back seat of the car could have been a sympathetic agreement to that possibility but it made Hanna smile again.

'Someone's waking up.'

'Which means they'll both be awake in about ten seconds flat. Shall we take them in? I think we've been spotted.'

Sure enough, the front door of the little house was opening by the time Hanna and Mac got out of the car and opened the back doors to unbuckle the restraints in the child car seats on either side. A woman with curly, white hair and a huge smile on her face came down the path between the dahlia bushes with a speed that was impressive for someone who was well into her eighties.

'You're here already,' she said.

'We are.' Hanna was reaching into the car to lift a young girl with a riot of red curls from the seat. 'How are you, Maureen?'

'All the better for seeing you.' She opened the gate. 'Oh, my… Haven't you grown, Ella?'

Hanna put the just-awake toddler down and she ran straight towards the older woman, holding her arms up. Maureen ruffled the flame-coloured ringlets and bent down for a kiss.

'How was the drive?' she asked Mac when she straightened, a tiny hand now holding hers and tugging her towards the house.

'In, Granny. *In…*'

'It's always a pleasure,' Mac said. 'I love the countryside between Dunedin and Oamaru. You get those gorgeous sea views and those lovely hills. Let's get inside and I'll show you the photos. Come on, wee man.' He lifted a still-sleepy boy from his seat.

'They've both grown so much,' Maureen said, a short time later. The twins were now wide awake and busy finding all their favourite toys that were in the big basket in the living room.

'Like weeds,' Hanna agreed. She sat down on the couch beside Maureen. 'I'm run ragged. It's good to have a break before we get to the next part of our day.'

Maureen laughed. 'You're clearly thriving on it, love. Does my heart good to see. Now, tell me everything that's been going on.'

Mac hadn't sat down yet. Like the very first time he'd been in this room, he was standing beside the window. Not because he was too nervous to sit down, this time, but because it was a touchstone to look out into the back garden of this home and see the old fruit trees and the swing that his sister, Jenny, had played on so many years ago. He would never forget the relief of how obvious it was that she had been a very much-loved child and that her sadly short life had been a very happy one.

There were dozens of photographs of Jenny at various ages around this room, from a tiny heart-shaped frame of her as a baby on the mantelpiece to a framed image of her just before she became sick, a gorgeous young teenager, with her long dark hair and eyes that were so like Mac's he'd felt a shiver down his spine the first time he'd seen it. No wonder it had been such a shock for Maureen when he'd turned up on her doorstep

252 ONE WEEKEND IN PRAGUE

that first time, even though they'd been in contact and she was expecting him.

'If only we'd known that Jenny was one of twins,' she'd told him that day, with tears streaming down her cheeks. 'We would have taken both of you in a heartbeat. I'm so sad my Jack isn't here to meet you now. He would've been over the moon to have a son. Not that we didn't both adore our Jenny, of course…'

That picture still gave him a frisson of something that couldn't be explained. It wasn't simply that he and Jenny had looked so alike. It was also that that particular photograph had been taken with a background of the Elephant Rocks.

'Her favourite place,' Maureen had told Mac and Hanna. 'We had all our family picnics there for so many years.'

The sound of his children's delight in the toys and the conversation between Maureen and Hanna became a background blur as Mac's gaze shifted to a much more recent photograph that was also framed and hanging on Maureen's wall. It had the same background with the distinctive shapes of those rocks—the herd of elephants gathered in their soft, grassy haven. There were quite a few people in this photo, however. He was in the centre, wearing his best kilt and Hanna was beside him in the most beautiful wedding dress he'd ever seen. Cade and Jo were there, having been the best man and maid of honour for their wedding, and Oli was holding her basket of petals upside down over her head.

Maureen was there too, of course. Tucked into the line-up on Mac's side. She might not have had the opportunity to adopt him as her son from the start, but she wasn't going to let that make any difference to how she felt about her beloved daughter's twin brother. Or to her sheer joy in becoming a grandmother to Liam and Ella, thanks to the wonderful surrogate that had helped create a miracle for Hanna and Mac.

He shifted his gaze again, away from the photos to the real people in this room.

His family.

A mother figure that was filling a bigger gap in his life than she would ever realise.

Two amazing children that he loved so much it could bring a lump to his throat just watching them like this.

And his wife…

Hanna.

The woman who'd changed his entire life, filling it with light and love and…adventures. Every day was an adventure. And, okay…maybe some of them didn't turn out quite how they might have wanted but that didn't matter, did it? If Mac had learned one thing over the last, amazing years with Hanna, it was that he'd been quite wrong to assume that keeping control of your life and being emotionally *safe* was the same thing as being *happy*.

What better way to celebrate their wedding anniversary than to continue what was becoming an annual event—a picnic visit to the place he'd discovered for them by following his own nose for once in his life. When he'd crashed that car and almost literally pushed them into a future he might never have otherwise dreamed of.

Thanks to that adventure going awry but mainly thanks to Hanna, Mac had learned what real happiness was like.

As if she felt his gaze, Hanna looked up and then held his gaze and Mac could feel that contact like a physical touch. Like the way he'd felt when she'd taken hold of his hand on the bus that day.

As if he'd found the way home even though he hadn't been looking for it.

Even then, he'd known he didn't want to waste a moment of the time he could have with this woman. But, if he'd known he was going to be lucky enough to be with her for the rest of his life, that wouldn't have changed anything.

He was always going to make the most of every moment with her. Including this one.

Hanna was still holding his gaze. It seemed like she was reading his thoughts at the same time because she was getting to her feet. Coming towards him.

'Happy anniversary,' she whispered when she was close. 'I love you.' Her eyes were shining with that love. 'Fancy a family picnic?'

* * * * *

If you enjoyed this story, check out these other great reads from Alison Roberts

A Paramedic to Change Her Life
Miracle Baby, Miracle Family
The Vet's Unexpected Family
Christmas Miracle at the Castle

All available now!